William Pitt, Christopher Wyvill

The Correspondence of the Rev. C. Wyvill with the Right Honourable William Pitt

published by Mr. Wyvill. Second Edition, Part 1

William Pitt, Christopher Wyvill

The Correspondence of the Rev. C. Wyvill with the Right Honourable William Pitt
published by Mr. Wyvill. Second Edition, Part 1

ISBN/EAN: 9783337195625

Printed in Europe, USA, Canada, Australia, Japan

Cover: Foto ©Andreas Hilbeck / pixelio.de

More available books at **www.hansebooks.com**

THE

CORRESPONDENCE

OF THE

REV. C. WYVILL

WITH THE

RIGHT HONOURABLE WILLIAM PITT.

⚜

PART I.

THE SECOND EDITION.

⚜

PUBLISHED BY MR WYVILL.

NEWCASTLE:

PRINTED BY S. HODGSON.

SOLD BY J. JOHNSON, LONDON, AND J. TODD, YORK.

1796.

ADVERTISEMENT.

THE publication of the Second Part of this Correſpondence is poſtponed. It will conſiſt of the following Papers:

1. Heads of a Bill, or Bills, for amending the Repreſentation.

2. Letter from the Right Honourable William Pitt to the Rev. C. Wyvill, incloſing a Sketch of a Preamble to the Bill.

3. The Sketch of a Preamble to the Bill.

4. Correƈted Clauſes by the Rev. C. Wyvill.

5. Ditto.

6. Ditto.

Paper I.

The substance of MR WYVILL's *conversation with* MR PITT, *on the 5th of May,* 1783; *communicated to the* Committee *of* Association *of the* County *of* York, *at their* Meeting, *on the* 1st *of Oct.* 1783.*

AFTER Mr Pitt had informed me what his motions on the 7th of May would be, I told him, I much approved the Proposition for preventing Bribery and Expence at Elections, and that for punishing Boroughs with disfranchisement on the conviction of a majority of the Electors having been guilty of corruption.—Respecting the third Proposition, for adding one hundred Members to the Counties and the Metropolis, I begged to know, whether it was his meaning that the proposed augmentation of Members should be made according to the proportion between England and Scotland, as established at the Union; and whether it was his meaning that the Members should be added in equal numbers

* At this Meeting, the Committee passed Resolutions, thanking Mr Pitt for his excellent proposition to Parliament on the 7th of May, 1783; and expressing their hopes of success from his virtuous perseverance.

A   to

to the feveral Counties, or in a due proportion
according to their refpective population and importance.—Mr Pitt affured me that it was his
idea, that the proportion agreed between England
and Scotland at the Union fhould be obferved in
the Diftribution of the Members; but that with
regard to the other meafure, viz. the mode of
diftribution to the feveral Counties, he was not
determined. It was in his own opinion proper
to make the augmentation in a due proportion
to the importance of each County; but feveral
of his friends were inclined to make it, by fimply
adding one or two to each County, without any
regard to population or fize. He feemed to wifh
for my opinion; I therefore told him, I was glad
to find his own Judgment led him to make the
propofed addition in due proportion, and earneft-
ly preffed him to abide by it.—The Nation felt
the inconvenience arifing from the want of fore-
fight in our forefathers, from whofe inatten-
tion to eftablifh and maintain due proportion
in the Houfe of Commons, the prefent complaints
of the People arofe. That it behoved us therefore to pay greater attention to Theory than they
had done; and to make the diftribution with a
regard to the importance of the Counties. There
might be local reafons, refpecting the Land-tax,
why the Members of fome parts of England,
Bedfordfhire for inftance, might wifh the addition fhould be made equally to each County,
without regard to its fize, &c.; but fince what
would gain thofe Members, for oppofite local reafons, would difguft the Members of other parts
of the kingdom, there was no advantage likely to
refult

result from it, in favour of the Plan, which could render it neceſſary or politic to ſacrifice Theory to greater Practicability. But what ſtruck me moſt forcibly, as an objection to adding an equal number of Members to the ſmall as well as the great Counties, was this, in the ſmall Counties the intereſt of powerful families is found moſt prevalent, in the large Counties the Democracy has uſually the greateſt weight; therefore, adding to the large Counties a proportionably large number of Members, would ſtrengthen the Democracy; whereas, adding as many to the ſmall Counties as to the large, would in a much greater degree ſtrengthen the Ariſtocracy, who are already too powerful in this Country, and the People too little ſo. In my opinion, therefore, the merit of the meaſure of adding more County members, depends greatly on its being done in due proportion.—This obſervation had the effect I deſired with Mr Pitt; and he determined to declare his opinion in the Houſe, on the 7th of May, that the augmentation ſhould be made *in due proportion.*—I then ventured to ſuggeſt to Mr Pitt, that as there were ſeveral great unrepreſented Towns, it ſtruck me, that when any corrupt Borough, in conſequence of his intended Regulation, was disfranchiſed, inſtead of ſinking the number of the Houſe of Commons, it might not be improper to transfer the Election Franchiſe to thoſe Towns; eſpecially, as otherwiſe the proportion between England and Scotland, which he wiſhed to have maintained, muſt probably be very ſoon broken through to a conſiderable degree. But as Mr Pitt wiſhed to obviate objections to in-

creaſing

creafing the number of Members, by providing means for their gradual decreafe again, what I obferved on this head did not meet his ideas. I alfo hinted, that his plan would be better received in the Capital, if in the courfe of his Speech he took occafion to mention, that the addition to the Capital would chiefly go to the unreprefented Inhabitants of Marybone, Pancras, Tower Hamlets, &c. But though he feemed to concur in fentiment, he did not chufe to touch upon the cafe of unreprefented Perfons, but to keep the fubject as clear as poffible in the outfet of any matter that could give offence. He feemed perfectly aware of the apprehenfions entertained concerning the Duke of Richmond's Plan, and refolved to avoid any thing that might bear the moft diftant conftruction of having a tendency that way.—I then told Mr Pitt how much I approved his whole Plan, as now explained, and my opinion, that it would be generally approved in Yorkfhire, as being full as much as they had any reafon to expect he would propofe to Parliament. The Regulation refpecting the Disfranchifement of corrupt Boroughs appeared to me particularly happy. And I thought, if his three propofitions were carried into effect, and the Septennial Bill was repealed, the objects of the Yorkfhire Affociation would be attained, and the County would probably determine to diffolve the Committee.

I was happy to find Mr Pitt was impreffed with fentiments of great refpect for the character and conduct of the Yorkfhire Gentlemen.

C. WYVILL.

Paper II.

LETTER *from the* Rev. C. WYVILL *to the* Right Honourable WILLIAM PITT.

KNIGHTSBRIDGE, *May* 23*d*, 1783.

Sir,

WHEN you did me the honour, on the 5th inftant, to explain your views in framing the three propofitions which were fubmitted to the confideration of Parliament on the 7th inft. I had no hefitation to declare my hearty approbation of your Plan. · In my apprehenfion, thofe propofitions were judicioufly adapted to the prefent ftate of Public Opinion, and were calculated to procure the beft and moft extenfive Reformation of Parliament, which could then be propofed with any probability of fuccefs, or on any fufficient ground of popular Declaration. If Parliament had confented to add one hundred Members to the Counties and the Metropolis, and to eftablifh Regulations for the prevention of Bribery and Expence at Elections, and for the Disfranchifement of Boroughs guilty of grofs and general Corruption, by thofe Improvements of the Conftitution, and the Repeal of the Septennial Bill, the objects of the Affociation of the County of York would have been completely attained, and in fome refpects exceeded. The admiffion of Copyholders to the Right of Election, the abolition of fictitious Votes in Scotland, and the Correc-

tion

tion of inferior, local, abufes of Election, might be expected to follow that Renovation of the Conftitution, without any farther interpofition of the People, by their Committees. And if the means thus provided for checking grofs Corruption fhould hereafter be found inadequate to that purpofe, and the decayed and venal Boroughs fhould ftill endanger the Liberty of the Nation, it is evident, that after every milder method of correction had failed to fecure the freedom and independence of Parliament, the AMPUTATION of thofe Boroughs, by an Act of the Legiflature, on due application from the People, would be a meafure perfectly unexceptionable, and alfo practicable with much greater facility than it can be thought at prefent. On thefe grounds I ventured to declare to you my firm perfuafion that, if your Propofitions fhould be adopted by Parliament, and the Septennial Bill fhould be repealed, that Parliamentary Reformation would be fatisfactory to the County of York, and the Committee would probably be diffolved at the next General Meeting of the County. As far as I could form a judgment of the difpofition of fo large a Body of Men, this appeared to me moft confiftent with their ufual candour and moderation; and I am happy to affure you, Sir, from fubfequent correfpondence, I am fatisfied, I did not materially mifreprefent their fentiments.

But I truft the opinion ftated to you, what in that cafe probably would be their conduct, was fufficiently underftood to bear an immediate reference to the actual circumftances of the county,

at

at that time only. Parliament, by rejecting your Plan, has in effect refused any redress of that national grievance, the gross inequality of the Representation of the People, of which the County of York, and many other great and important Districts, had complained. The refusal loudly calls upon those Bodies to reiterate their application to Parliament, and to press with increasing vigour for a due correction of that alarming abuse. If, therefore, in the course of this unavoidable struggle, the Yorkshire Gentlemen shall be supported by a more general concurrence of their fellow-citizens, and terms of greater advantage to the Constitution, than those which Parliament has so recently rejected, shall appear to be attainable by regular and legal means, in justice to themselves, in justice to the Public, and to Posterity, they will not stop short at inferior Improvements. But the County of York, far from wishing to push the Reformation of Parliament to an indefinite extent, has guarded against the possibility of that excess, by its Resolutions on the 19th of December, 1782. There the County has drawn a line, beyond which, in my conception, it stands pledged not to proceed; but within those limits it certainly may be expected to exert strenuous efforts to obtain the best possible security for the Rights and Liberty of the Nation.

Feeling, as they do, the utmost gratitude for your generous, though hitherto unsuccessful, endeavours to Restore the Constitution, I am persuaded the Yorkshire Gentlemen will, with perfect confidence, rely on your zeal to promote

A 4   the

the moſt effectual Reformation of Parliament
which, in any future ſituation of the Country,
may be found practicable.

I have the honour to be,

With high reſpect, Sir,

Your moſt obedient ſervant,

C. WYVILL.

Paper III.

The Subſtance *of* Mr WYVILL's Converſation
with the Right Hon. W. PITT, *February* 15th,
1784; *communicated to the* Yorkſhire Gentlemen *alluded to in it.*

I Told Mr Pitt that I wiſhed for an opportunity
to inform him what was paſſing in Yorkſhire,
on the ſubject of an Addreſs to the Throne: that
a Requiſition to the Sheriff, for a County Meeting to be called for that purpoſe, had been
ſigned about ten days ago by a few Gentlemen
in the Weſt-Riding; that their number was now
increaſed to fifty-four; and as it ſeemed agreeable to the ſenſe of that part of the County, that
there was little doubt the meaſure would take
place. I mentioned my own general approbation
of it; but that I thought there might be ſome
danger from running precipitately into an Addreſs

drefs on the fubject of Prerogative; there might be future inconvenience from it; and, therefore, in concurrence with other Gentlemen, I wifhed the queftion there to be, an Addrefs for the Diffolution of Parliament. On this fubject Mr Pitt expreffed fome difficulties; declared his intention, however, not to agree to any conciliation with the better part of his opponents, unlefs the India Bill, as calculated to eftablifh a new Executive Power, was given up; and alfo fuch other meafures as had a fimilar tendency; but thought it now plain, that let Government change hands as it might, thofe dangerous meafures muft be defeated. On this, I told Mr Pitt how much I had rejoiced at the part he had taken in oppofing the India Bill, and that I had no doubt the public would fupport him in requiring that meafure to be given up: that as to the difficulties attending a Diffolution of Parliament, I was aware of them; but if the fupplies were ftopt, if the annual Mutiny Bill was rejected, if public bufinefs was ftill obftructed, in that cafe a Diffolution of Parliament feemed to be perfectly juftifiable,* as the only conftitutional meafure by which Government could be fupported: that the Meeting of the County of York would probably not take place for three weeks, in order to give time for thefe matters to be afcertained. If Union on the ground fpecified by Mr Pitt was

---

* The idea here fuggefted was adopted by the Meeting of the County of York on the 25th of March, 1784; in whofe Petition it may be found expanded, and at large infifted on, at the 327th page of the 2d volume of Political Papers.

at

at all attainable, it probably would be attained
within that time; and the Supplies, the Mutiny
Bill, &c. would be decided.

On the subject of Union, Mr Pitt agreed it
must take place soon, or not at all; considering
the manner in which he had been treated, it
could not be supposed that Union could be particularly pleasant to him ; but that for the Public
Good he thought it would be right to agree to
it, on the terms already mentioned: that Lord
North was now out of the question, and therefore
a Union with the better part of the Opposition
was what he had some hope of, though he could
not be very sanguine in his expectations of it.

C. WYViLL.

Paper IV.

Letter *from the* Rev. C. Wyvill *to the* Right
Honourable William Pitt.

York Tavern, April 3, 1784.

Dear Sir,

I Received last night the honour of your Letter
from Mr Wilberforce, just after the Nomination Meeting had been closed by the Sheriff's
declaration of a very considerable majority of
hands in favour of Mr Duncombe and Mr Wilberforce. I was aware, from the beginning of
this

this bufinefs, that great prejudices againft the Affociation fubfifted in the minds of many Gentlemen here, who are Friends to your Adminiftration; and, on my own part, have found it extremely difficult to avoid roufing thofe perfonal
refentments againft myfelf, which my former
conduct had excited, and my prefent had not
extinguifhed. It was not poffible to avoid a public difcuffion of the topic of the Affociation, not
indeed at the County Meeting, but, however, at.
a very large Meeting of our Confederate Friends
on the evening of the 26th of March. The difcuffion ended in mutual fatisfaction, and, I hope,
a total difmiffion of the jealoufies which had
been conceived, and which threatened a breach
that muft have rendered any attempt to difplace
Mr Foljambe totally impracticable. The next day
(the 27th of March) it was refolved to call the
Meeting held yefterday for the nomination of Can-
didates; and the whole of the bufinefs ever fince
has been conducted with perfect cordiality, both
in our private Meetings, and alfo at the Great
Meeting of the County yefterday. From the general attendance of the Freeholders, without foli-
citation on our part, and the warmth with which
the joint nomination of Meffrs Duncombe and
Wilberforce was fupported by them, I have no
doubt the fenfe of the County is decidedly in our
favour; and though violent efforts will be made
againft our Friends, and the moft compulfive
means will be ufed to influence every perfon in
any degree dependent on our adverfaries, yet
final fuccefs in the County Election, I think, may
be

be depended on. Lord John* is in great danger of being thrown out of this City; and a report has juſt reached this place, that the Devonſhire Nomination at Knareſborough, by ſome ſtrange fortuitous concurrence of circumſtances, has been defeated, and Sir John Coghill and Mr Bacon Frank have been returned for that place. However, I think it probable there is ſome miſtake in this report.---The Subſcription † for ſupporting the Election amounts to more than 20,000 l. excluſive of what may have been ſubſcribed in London.

I am, Sir, with moſt ſincere reſpect,

Your faithful and obedient ſervant,

C. WYVILL.

* Lord John Cavendiſh.

† This Subſcription was intended to defray the unavoidable expence, as the Law now ſtands, of a conteſted Election for the County of York; an expence by far too great for the purſe of any candidate, however opulent. The magnitude of the legal expence at conteſted Elections for counties or great towns aggravates the evil conſequences of the defects in our Repreſentation, by diſabling the ſound parts of the Conſtituent Body duly to exerciſe their important Right of Election. It is a regulation of the firſt neceſſity, that ſuch expence at conteſted Elections be prevented, whether our Repreſentation be amended, or be ſuffered to remain in its preſent groſsly defective ſtate.

N. B. Mr Pitt's Letter to the Editor, dated March 30th, 1784, to which the preceding Letter is an anſwer, is not produced, becauſe the Letter and its Cover are both indorſed by Mr Pitt, "Private."—For a ſimilar reaſon, Mr Pitt's anſwer to the preceding Letter, dated April 6, 1784, is ſuppreſſed.—For nearly the ſame reaſon, ſome of Sir G. Savile's Letters to the Editor were before deemed inadmiſſible, when he was forming the Collection of Political Papers lately publiſhed.

It ſeems not improper here to ſtate, that not one of the other papers written by Mr Pitt, and contained in this publication, is indorſed by him, "Private;" as the two Letters are indorſed, which are ſuppreſſed.

Paper V.

Paper V.

Letter *from the* Rev. C. WYVILL *to the* Right Honourable WILLIAM PITT.

NEROT's HOTEL, *Jan.* 20, 1785.

Dear Sir,

THE Newfpapers abound with malevolent paragraphs on the fubject of your intention to fupport the Reform of our Reprefentation, *as a Minifter ;* * a fpecimen of which I inclofe for your perufal, together with my reply to it, and, alfo, my reply to other paragraphs of the fame tendency, which have appeared in a different paper.

I do affure you, that I am perfectly fatisfied every thing is rightly underftood between us.

* If any of the Replies to the malevolent paragraphs, here alluded to, had been preferved, they would not have been withheld from the Reader. The Circular Letter, which the Editor addreffed to the Friends of Political Reformation throughout Great Britain, announcing Mr Pitt's intention to fupport their Caufe, *as a Minifter and a Man,* was written with Mr Pitt's confent, at the Editor's requeft, with a view to animate them, and obtain the general fuppoit of the People, in County Meetings, &c.: And from Mr Pitt's compliance with this requeft, as well as from other parts of his conduct, the fincerity of his attachment to the caufe of Reformation, *at this time,* feems to be unqueftionable. It is due to Mr Pitt to add, that when this Circular Letter became, foon after the date of it, the fubject of animadverfion in Parliament, and was there treated by fome as an unauthorized Letter, and confidered by others as a Letter authentic indeed, but conceived in very exceptionable Terms, Mr Pitt did Mr Wyvill ample juftice, declaring, that the Letter was written with his confent ; and though not dictated by him, truly and well expreffed what he meant to have faid.

You

You have placed in me a * Truſt of the greateſt conſequence; and I am conſcious of having acted in it with fidelity, to the beſt of my Judgment. On the other hand, I have acted thus, without a ſingle ſcrap of paper, or written authority of any kind. This is, I confeſs, a ſlender return for your confidence in me; but it was the beſt return in my power.—I have only to add upon this ſubject, that I wiſh to have no written anſwer to this Note; I never wanted it before, nor do I now deſire it. If I had it in my power to expreſs a more full reliance, I would.

The other incloſed Papers are copies of my earlieſt Letters, on the ſubject of our converſation, to Mr Maſon, Mr Tooker, and Mr Wilkinſon; † that to Lord Effingham I have not yet obtained.

Believe me ever, dear Sir,

With the higheſt regard,

Moſt faithfully your's,

C. WYVILL.

* The Truſt here alluded to, was the authority verbally given to Mr Wyvill by Mr Pitt, to communicate to the Friends of Reformation, as widely as poſſible, his intention to promote their Cauſe to the utmoſt extent of his power; and to invite their aſſiſtance by Petitions at General Meetings, &c. Copies of the moſt material Letters which had been written by the Editor, on this ſubject, were at this time ſeen and approved by Mr Pitt.

The Paper, intitled, "Heads of a Bill or Bills for amending the Repreſentation," was intruſted with Mr Wyvill, probably, ſoon after this time; but of the day when it was delivered to him, he has found no mention.

† For a Copy of the Letter to Mr Wilkinſon, here alluded to, and for Copies of ſome other Letters on the ſame ſubject, ſee the Appendix.

Paper VI.

Paper VI.

Letter *from the* Right Honourable WILLIAM
PITT *to the* Rev. C. WYVILL.

Monday (suppofed to be Monday the 24th
of January, 1785.)

My dear Sir,

IN reconfidering the fubject on which I had
the pleafure of converfing with you, I fee no
reafon to vary the opinion in which we then
agreed as to the propriety of a Meeting.*
Believe me, dear Sir,
Faithfully and fincerely your's,
W. PITT.

* The Meeting alluded to in this Letter was that Meeting of
the County of York which was held on Thurfday the 10th of
February, 1785, in order to give their utmoft fupport to Mr
Pitt's intended Motion in Parliament, for effecting a Reform in
the Reprefentation. The Circular Letter mentioned in the firft
note annexed to Paper V. had inclined the major part of the
Yorkfhire Committee to affemble the County for this purpofe:
fome, however, of the moft refpectable Members of the Committee, whofe attachment to the caufe of Reformation was
undoubted, were averfe from the meafure, fearing that the appearance of diminifhed zeal might injure the caufe, if the propofed Meeting fhould be lefs numeroufly attended than fimilar
Meetings had been attended before. From this Letter it may
be collected, that after due deliberation, Mr Pitt gave the fanc-
tion of his decided approbation to the meafure of a County
Meeting. The Circular Letter had been agreed to, with a view
to obtain, if poffible, a Declaration from the Collective Body of
the People in favour of the intended Reform. Under the circumftances which have been ftated, Mr Pitt's perfeverance to
act in purfuance of the plan laid down, affords another proof of
his fincere attachment, *at this time*, to the caufe of Reformation.

Paper VII.

Paper VII.

LETTER *from the* Rev. C. WYVILL *to the* Right Honourable WILLIAM PITT.

NEROT'S HOTEL, *Feb.* 2, 1785.

Dear Sir,

I Beg leave for a moment, to interrupt you, juft to fay, that on Saturday next, at an early hour, I fhall fet out for York; and to remind you, that fome points of real importance, refpecting the Yorkfhire Meeting, are yet unarranged. I have no doubt of our fuperiority there; but I believe you agree with me in thinking, it is very much the intereft of the Common Caufe to render that fuperiority as great and decifive as poffible.

I am, dear Sir,
With the higheft refpect and regard,
Your faithful humble fervant,
C. WYVILL.

Paper VIII.

Paper VIII.

Letter *from the* Right Honourable WILLIAM PITT *to the* Rev. C. WYVILL.

DOWNING-STREET, *Feb.* 16*th,* 1785.

My dear Sir,

I Have but one moment, of which, however, I cannot omit making ufe, to return you many thanks for your * Two Letters, and to congratulate you on the fuccefs which has fo amply juftified your expectation. I truft this happy example will have a powerful and general effect.

I am, with great truth and regard,
Dear Sir,
Your moft faithful and obedient
W. PITT.

* Copies of the two Letters here alluded to have not been preferved. They probably contained a particular account of proceedings at a previous Meeting on the 9th of February, and at the General Meeting of the County of York on the 10th of February, 1785. On this occafion, the expectations of general fupport throughout the kingdom, formed by the Minifter and his Friends, were unfortunately difappointed; the laudable example of the County of York was not followed with vigour by the reft of the nation: few Petitions were prefented to Parliament; the zeal, tranfcendent abilities, and influence of Mr Pitt, were unable, without a ftrong concurrence of the people, to check the habitual tendency of the fyftem; ill fupported by them, his mild and prudent propofal of Reformation neceffarily fell to the ground.

Paper IX.

Paper IX.

Letter *from the* Rev. C. WYVILL *to the* Right
Honourable WILLIAM PITT.

NEROT's HOTEL, *Feb. 28th,* 1785.

Dear Sir,

WHEN I lately mentioned the money accu-
mulated in the hands of the Governors
of Queen Anne's Bounty, as a fum that on certain conditions might be juftly applied to the
fervice of the State, you feemed to think the
fubject deferved farther confideration. The inclofed Propofal* is the refult of what has occurred to me; and, without pretending to any
financial fkill, I fhall much rejoice, if you find it
capable of being turned to any ferviceable purpofe.

I am ever, with the greateft regard,
Dear Sir,
Your moft faithful humble fervant,
C. WYVILL.

* The Memorial at page 19 contains this Propofal.

Paper X.

Paper X.

MEMORIAL *respecting* certain Sums *of* Money *vested in the* Governors *of* Queen Anne's Bounty; *and the* conditions *on which the said* Sums *seem justly applicable to the* Public Service.

IT is underſtood, that the Governors of Queen Anne's Bounty are poſſeſſed of one conſiderable ſum of money veſted in their names, or in truſt to them, though appropriated to augment certain ſmall benefices in England and Wales. For this ſum, intereſt not exceeding 2 per cent. is annually paid to the ſeveral incumbents of thoſe benefices, according to their reſpective appropriated ſhares. It is alſo underſtood, that another large ſum is veſted in the ſaid Governors, which is wholly unappropriated. The total accumulation of theſe monies, appropriated and unappropriated, may be taken to amount to 500,000 l.

The excuſe which is alledged for this accumulation is, the extreme difficulty of finding purchaſable Lands of the exact value wanted, and perfectly unexceptionable in title, and every other reſpect. As 2 per cent. has been the annual allowance of intereſt for ſuch ſums as have been allotted to certain poor benefices, until eſtates could be purchaſed, and annexed to each benefice; and as few ſuch purchaſes have been made even during the laſt ten years, in which the price of land has been uncommonly low,

and

and confequently the incumbents of fuch poor benefices were interefted in a more than ufual degree to find proper eftates to be purchafed with their refpective allotments, the excufe alledged feems to be a fair and fufficient exculpation of the perfons concerned in this truft.

But the validity of their plea proves, that, under the prefent regulations, accumulation will be continued, and the relief of the poorer Clergy, the immediate purpofe of this benevolent Donation, will be much retarded, or rather, in many inftances, will be entirely defeated. It appears, therefore, to be not only juft and equitable, but neceffary for the due accomplifhments of augmentation intended by Queen Anne, that Parliament fhould interpofe, to direct an application of the faid fund in fome more fpeedy and effectual mode, to that charitable purpofe.

This being admitted to be proper, it is propofed, that Government fhall apply to Parliament for an Act, ordaining that the above-mentioned accumulation of money, fuppofed to amount to 500,000l. fhall be paid into the Exchequer at Midfummer next, on the conditions following; to wit:

1. That from the date of fuch transfer to the State, the Public Faith fhall be engaged to pay the intereft to become due for all appropriated fums as aforefaid, part of the faid 500,000l. at the rate of 2 per cent. per ann. till Michaelmas next, and from Michaelmas, for ever, at the rate of 5 per cent. per ann.

2. That returns of all the benefices in England and Wales, under 50l. per ann. fhall be exhibited

exhibited to Parliament within twenty days after the commencement of the next Seſſion, in order that intereſt at the rate of 5 per cent. per ann. for the unappropriated ſum, being the reſidue of the ſaid 500,000 l. may be diſtributed in ſuch manner as Parliament ſhall appoint for the augmentation of the ſaid benefices.

3. That the payment of Firſt-fruits and Tenths ſhall be continued for the farther augmentation of the ſaid benefices, *in this mode*, *annually*, until the income of every benefice ſhall have been augmented to 50 l. per ann. and no more. And when no benefice under 50 l. a year ſhall be left in England and Wales, the payment of Firſt-fruits and Tenths ſhall be then diſcontinued, and wholly extinguiſhed.

4. Laſtly, that a clauſe ſhall be added to every future Land-tax Aćt, directing the Receivers-General of the Land-tax in England and Wales, out of the monies collećted by virtue of ſuch Aćt, by half-yearly payments, and without fee or dedućtion whatſoever, to pay the ſums thus appropriated by Parliament to the incumbents of the ſeveral augmented benefices within their reſpećtive diſtrićts; or otherwiſe, to cauſe the ſaid ſums to be paid by ſuch Collećtors of the Land-tax within their reſpećtive diſtrićts, as may reſide neareſt to the place of reſidence of the ſaid incumbents.*

C. WYVILL.

London, *Feb. 26th*, 1785.

B 3

Paper XI.

---

* If the appropriation of the ſum of money mentioned in this Memorial had taken place on the terms propoſed, the State would

Paper XI.

Note *from the* Right Honourable WILLIAM PITT *to the* Rev. C. WYVILL.

MR Pitt prefents his compliments to Mr Wyvill, and if he is difengaged at nine on Friday morning, would be much obliged to him if he would take his Breakfaft in Downing-ftreet, as Mr Pitt wifhes much for the honour of feeing him* previous to Monday.

DOWNING-STREET, *Wednefday, April 13th.*

would have been accommodated with the loan of it on eafy intereft, and a great number of the inferior Clergymen of the Church of England, who are at once the moft neceffitous and the moft laborious Members of that Body, would have received a comfortable addition to their flender incomes If the fum in queftion be vefted entirely in the 3 per cent. Fund, it would have afforded an immediate increafe of 15l. a year to at leaft one thoufand of the moft indigent of our parochial Priefts: It would have afforded more if vefted in the other Funds; and the fums raifed in future by the operation of Queen Anne's Bounty, inftead of being fuffered again to accumulate into a large and ufelefs mafs, would have been applied as fpeedily as they poffibly could be, to the relief of the remaining poor parifh Priefts of the Church of England, till at laft, after the object of the Queen's Bounty had been fully attained, the taxes of Firft-fruits and Tenths, often found by the beneficed Clergy to be very inconvenient and burthenfome, would have been difcontinued.— If the principles of this propofal fhould be approved, the time may come, it even feems to be at no very great diftance, when the application of them may afford a fupply neither inconfiderable nor unfeafonable to the exigencies of the State.

* The object of this interview was farther confultation on the intended Motion for a Reform in the Reprefentation, previous to the day fixed for making it, viz. Monday, April 18th, 1785.

Paper XII.

Paper XII.

Letter *from the* Right Honourable WILLIAM PITT *to the* Rev. C. WYVILL.

DOWNING-STREET, *May 7th,* 1785.

Dear Sir,

I Flatter myself the Queen Anne's Bounty may be made useful to the Public Service, but I think it need not come as part of the Budget; which makes it unneceffary for me to trouble you immediately.

I fhall be extremely happy to fee you when the bufinefs of the prefent moment is a little over.   I am, dear Sir,
Your moft faithful
and obedient fervant,
W. PITT.

Paper XIII.

Letter *from the* Right Honourable WILLIAM PITT *to the* Rev. C. WYVILL.

PUTNEY-HEATH, *May 29th,* 1785.

Dear Sir,

BUSINESS which I muft difpatch before tomorrow, has obliged me, contrary to my

    inten-

intention, to ſtay here to-day. I cannot eaſily be in town ſooner than half paſt twelve to-morrow, and ſhould be very glad to have the pleaſure of ſeeing you then in Downing-ſtreet, if it is not inconvenient to you. But if the time of your ſetting out makes an early hour of conſequence, I will endeavour to meet you as much ſooner as you pleaſe.*

I am, dear Sir,

Very ſincerely your's,

W. PITT.

---

* At this time Mr Wyvill was on the point of paſſing over to the Continent, on an excurſion through Paris to the Glaciers of Savoy and Switzerland. Having been kindly furniſhed by Viſcount Mahon with a Letter of Introduction to Dr Franklin, Mr Wyvill wiſhed to inform Mr Pitt of this circumſtance, and to offer his ſervice, if he could be of any, during his intended ſhort reſidence at Paris. On his arrival in that capital, Mr Wyvill haſtened to pay his reſpects to the venerable Ambaſſador of America; by whom he was received with every mark of cordial civility and good-will. In repeated converſations with Mr Wyvill, Dr Franklin expreſſed his own amicable diſpoſition to Great-Britain; and his earneſt wiſh that the recent reconciliation between this country and America might be improved into the cloſeſt friendſhip and union, by the prudence, moderation, and good faith of their reſpective Governments.

Paper XIV.

Paper XIV.

Letter *from the* Rev. C. WYVILL *to the* Right Honourable WILLIAM PITT.

BURTON-HALL, *December 11th,* 1785.

Dear Sir,

MY Father has informed me that a Petition has lately been tranfmitted by him to the Board of Treafury, requefting that a Penfion, which he has enjoyed feveral years, may by their authority be continued; without which allowance, the Board of Excife in Scotland have intimated their intention to difcontinue it, as inconfiftent with the fpirit of the prefent Adminiftration.

On this occafion I fhould difapprove my own conduct, if I remained filent; becaufe I think it extremely probable, from the regard with which you have honoured me fo much, that you may feel fome difficulty, fome degree of reluctance, to enforce, in the prefent inftance, thofe frugal maxims of Government, which you have laid down with the fame ftrictnefs as you would carry them into execution in ordinary cafes. Permit me, therefore, to affure you, that it is my earneft and only wifh, that you will put me and my connection with the Petitioner entirely out of your confideration, and treat him exactly as you would treat every other perfon in the fame predicament. If the circumftances of his cafe do not juftify the penfion as an indulgence meri

ted

ted by fervice, unobjectionable in point of precedent, and fit to be allowed in all fimilar fituations,
it ought to be ftruck off; and I fhall applaud the
hand which does refcind it, with as much fincerity, and with as much alacrity too, as if the
perfon afflicted by the ftroke were altogether unknown to me. I fay this not from indifference
to fo near a relation, becaufe I mean to compen-
fate his lofs, as I had before promifed I would,
when, from the part I took in promoting a Petition to Parliament againft unmerited Penfions,
&c. it was not improbable *his* might be difallowed by the Minifter then, for reafons very different from thofe which I am certain will determine your refolution now. In preffing you to
put me quite out of the queftion, and to act
according to your impartial judgment alone, I
do what I conceive to be my duty; and I fhould
ill deferve your regard and good opinion, which
I value fo highly, if I could entertain a wifh for
a fingle moment, that, on my account, you
would depart from thofe general rules of œconomy, which are, in the prefent exhaufted ftate
of our country, indifpenfably neceffary.

I am, dear Sir,

With the greateft refpect and regard,
Moft faithfully your's,

C. WYVILL.

Paper XV.

Paper XV.

Letter *from the* Right Honourable WILLIAM
PITT *to the* Rev. C. WYVILL.

HOLWOOD-HILL, *Jan. 8th,* 1786.

Dear Sir,

I Meant to have acknowledged immediately
the favor of your Letter, and am extremely
concerned that in the variety of bufinefs it has
from time to time efcaped me. The fentiments
you exprefs are fuch as, from knowing your
character and principle, I cannot be furprized
at. It would, I confefs, have given me great
pain, if a perfon fo nearly connected with you
had been a fufferer by any fyftem laid down by
the prefent Government, however unavoidable.
I have, therefore, peculiar pleafure in being able
to affure you, that, before I received your Letter, or knew that Mr Wyvill had any connection
with you, the fimple circumftance of the cafe
had determined me to fend directions to the
Commiffioners of the Excife in Scotland to continue his Penfion, as being clearly not within
the line of a juft and rational reduction.—I hope
your health has benefited by your fummer exertions.*   Believe me to be at all times,
My dear Sir,
With the greateft regard,
Moft faithfully your's,
W. PITT.

* N. B. This is the laft Letter received by Mr Wyvill from
Mr Pitt.

Paper XVI.

Paper XVI.

Letter *from the* Rev. C. WYVILL *to the* Right Honourable WILLIAM PITT.

BURTON-HALL, *Jan.* 11th, 1787.

Dear Sir,

MR Wilberforce having lately expreſſed his intention to reſume, in the next Seſſion of Parliament, the ſubjeÛt of a County Regiſter, with ſome modification of Lord Stanhope's Plan;* and having yet formed no decided opinion what that modification ought to be, I have thrown together ſome thoughts upon it, which are communicated to him by this poſt; and I alſo venture to trouble you with a copy, though not without much heſitation, conſidering the near

* The principle of the modified Plan here alluded to, is, to employ the Conſtable to form, annually, a Liſt of the Freeholders within his townſhip who are qualified to vote at Elections for the County, as he is at preſent employed to form a Liſt of Freeholders qualified to ſerve as Jurors. Were the County Electors thus aſcertained, a great reduction of expence at Elections for the Counties might be effected; the poll might be taken at the chief place of every Hundred, or in every Pariſh, which would be ſtill better.—Whether this idea was or was not approved by Mr Pitt, is not certainly known to the Editor, by whom *no anſwer was received* to this Letter Mr Wilberforce approved and adopted the plan ſuggeſted, and placed it in the hands of the Editor's Friend, John Baynes, Eſq. a young Lawyer of the greateſt expectation, to be drawn by him in a technical form; but before he had drawn the Bill, Mr Baynes died. After his lamented death, the plan was ſaid to be communicated to A. Luders, Eſq. for the ſame purpoſe; but before he was able to finiſh this taſk, the death of Mr Phillips, the intended mover of the Bill, and the growing indiſpoſition of the Houſe of Commons to every queſtion of Reform, diſconcerted and finally defeated the deſign.

approach

approach of your bufieft feafon. I am aware how imperfect a fketch I now fubmit to your perufal; but if the propofed alteration in the paper inclofed fhould fortunately meet your opinion, and Mr Wilberforce and Lord Stanhope fhould be content to admit the modification, I think, when properly corrected, it might probably pafs both the Houfes of Parliament with lefs oppofition than his Lordfhip's Plan experienced laft year, as it is fomewhat lefs complicated, and fomewhat lefs remote from the common practice.—The only material objection which has occurred to myfelf, or thofe I have been able to confult, is, that the Conftable might abufe his power. In times of tranquillity, I am perfuaded, this would rarely happen; never, perhaps, to any dangerous extent. In times of much political agitation, if fome fhould be interefted. to tempt the Conftable to tranfgrefs, others would be found equally interefted to watch, and to detect the fraud.—No Schedule accompanies the Plan, though often referred to in it. In moft of thofe references, the regulations in Lord Stanhope's Schedule are what I had in view: But if the general idea fhould have your approbation, the Schedule, I fuppofe, would be eafily compleated.

It is with great pleafure I take this opportunity to affure you, that your relaxation* of the
Horfe-

* By this relaxation, farmers renting lefs than 70 pounds a year were exempted from paying the Horfe-tax. This exemption was propofed to Mr Pitt at an official interview by the Editor, with the concurrence of Mr Duncombe and Mr Wilberforce.— The Secretaries objected the precarious ftate of the Revenue, which

Horfe-tax laſt year has been received in this
country with that univerſal fatisfaction and gratitude, which an indulgence in itſelf ſo great,
and granted at a time ſo critical to your reputa-
tion as a Miniſter, ſo well deferved.

   I am, with the higheſt regard,
     Dear Sir,
       Your moſt faithful
        and obedient fervant,
          C. WYVILL.

***

Paper XVII.

Letter *from the* Rev. C. Wyvill *to the* Right
  Honourable William Pitt.

         Burton-Hall, *July 29th,* 1787.

Dear Sir,

* WHEN your Propofitions for reforming
   our Reprefentation were offered to the
Houfe of Commons, the diftrefsful confequences
              of

which at that time could ill bear ſo confiderable a defalcation.
But the propriety of relieving the pooreſt clafs of cultivators
from a burthen that ought only to fall on the rich proprietors
of horfes uſed for luxury, prevailed with Mr Pitt, and the defired indulgence was granted.—Mr Wyvill ſtates this circumſtance with pleaſure ; it does credit to the financial principles
and courage of Mr Pitt.

 * Two winters had paſſed after the laſt motion made by Mr
Pitt for amending our Reprefentation, and yet his expected
Bill was not produced. Whether this delay ought to be im-
               puted

of the War with America were yet felt feverely by the nation; and the corruption of Parliament, under a former Minister, was yet confidered, with general deteftation, as the principal caufe of thofe misfortunes. But the adoption of your whole fyftem feems to be referved for fome period of ftill greater-diftrefs, when the abufes of corruption fhall have been more ruinoufly practifed, and fhall have rendered the change more evidently and more indifpenfably neceffary. For, even at that time, the majority of the people, as well as of the Houfe of Commons, appears to have been adverfe to your propofai; not, probably, from any fixed difapprobation

puted to caution or inadvertence, to a prefs of official bufinefs, or a nafcent change in the Minifter's fyftem about this time, it is not eafy to determine. But it is certain the delay much exceeded the time within which the appearance of the Bill was looked for by the Friends of Reformation. The fincerity of their Leader, however, was not then fufpected by the Editor; though he thought it his duty to remind Mr Pitt, that the publication of his Bill was expected. Some peculiar circumftances relative to a borough, dependent on the Board of Ordnance, feemed to prefent a favourable opportunity for its publication at that time. But to the Editor's Letter ftating thefe confiderations to Mr Pitt, with the accuftomed freedom of their former intercourfe, yet with all becoming deference and friendly zeal for the honour of his character, *no anfwer was returned.*

Some furprize, and fome flight jealoufies, were the natural confequence of this filence; but they foon yielded to the ftrong prepoffeffion in Mr Pitt's favour. Within a few years after this period, however, the original principles of his Adminiftration feemed to have been abandoned, and a fyftem lefs pure, lefs œconomical, lefs friendly to popular rights, began to be gradually unfolded. But confidence once given, frankly and fincerely. is flowly and reluctantly withdrawn; and it was not till many years after the date of this Letter that the Editor was at laft convinced, by the tenor of Mr Pitt's conduct, that he was become unfaithful to the caufe in which he had engaged himfelf.

of

of the Plan itfelf, but becaufe the Peace had
already leffened in fome degree the preffure of
calamity, and the profpect of happier times had
produced a difpofition to acquiefce. Since the
rejection of that motion, the profperity of the
country has been advanced with a rapidity beyond all expectation; Trade has increafed,
Stocks have rifen, the Finances have been re-
duced into good order, and Government has
been fteadily conducted on the principles of virtuous œconomy. In its eagernefs to enjoy thefe
bleffings, the nation forgets their precarious te-
nure; and as the benefits of your Adminiftration
are more extenfively experienced, it feems more
generally difinclined to any great Parliamentary
change, though recommended even by your authority.

In this ftate of affairs, and in this temper of
the nation, I truft there is not a Zealot fo rafh
and intemperate in his purfuit of Political Reformation, as to wifh you to agitate that fubject
again in Parliament. Be that, however, as it
may, I certainly have not the fmalleft intention
to trouble you with any fuch unfeafonable fuggeftions. I only beg leave to recall to your
remembrance a meafure which I ventured to
propofe juft after the lofs of your great queftion.
You then expreffed your approbation of the
idea, that an authentic publication of your intended Bill was due to the public, and to your
own character. At that juncture, it was neither
neceffary, nor indeed prudent, to carry this
meafure into immediate execution. All the in-
formation on the fubject which could at that
time

time be given with propriety, was communicated to the public in the Summary Explanation
of its principles, which I had the honour to publish with your permiffion.* But, as your other
important plans for the good of your country
had not yet received their difcuffion and decifion, the publication of the Bill in queftion was

* This paffage alludes to a fact which at the date of this
Letter was recent, and all the material circumftances of which
were undoubtedly frefh in the recollection of Mr Pitt. Hence
the brevity of the expreffion, which renders the meaning fomewhat obfcure. The fact alluded to was this; the Summary Explanation was written with Mr Pitt's previous affent, in order
to be laid before the Meeting at the Thatched Houfe on the
24th of May, 1785, as the ground on which they might proceed to the confideration of the merits of his plan: And Mr
Pitt's affent had been given exprefsly on condition that the
piece fhould contain no allufion to the Heads of his Bill. The
Summary Explanation was written in conformity with this condition; it was feen by Mr Pitt, and he gave Mr Wyvill his
permiffion to publifh it, to lay it before the Meeting, and to
declare that Mr Pitt acknowledged the Explanation to be an
accurate account of the principles of that fyftem of Reform
which he had recommended to Parliament on the 18th of April,
1785. Concerning the Paper intitled Heads of a Bill, or Bills
for amending the Reprefentation, it may be proper here to ob-
ferve, that,

1. The Heads, &c. were delivered to Mr Wyvill by Mr Pitt,
fome time before the 18th of April, 1785, without any condition or referve at the time expreffed or underftood.

2. That in May 1785, Mr Pitt, for reafons of a temporary
nature, required, and Mr Wyvill promifed, that there fhould
be no allufion to the Heads, &c. in the Summary Explanation.

3. That the promife was *literally* fulfilled, by the omiffion of
any allufion to the Heads in the Summary Explanation; and *in
fpirit*, by the Editor's filence upon the fubject till the year 1793,
when the circumftances which rendered that referve neceffary
had long ceafed to exift.

4. That no promife of fecrecy, or referve of any kind, was
required by Mr Pitt, or agreed to by Mr Wyvill, refpecting any
other Papers which paffed between them, except only the two
Letters indorfed *Private*, which are not intended for publication.

C   very

very properly poftponed, till you had leifure to reconfider the ftate of our Reprefentation, and to correct your draught with that care and accuracy which the extreme importance of the fubject demands. Whether the moment of leifure be now arrived, or be ftill at fome diftance, is more than I pretend to judge; yet, if the commotions in Holland, which have threatened to embroil us with that Province and with France, fhould be fortunately compofed by your prudence and firmnefs, it is poffible that the prefent recefs may afford the opportunity which is wanted to prepare fuch a Bill for publication.

In my thoughts, there are various perfonal and public motives for the execution of this meafure during your continuance in power; and to narrow the idea ftill more, during the exiftence of the prefent Parliament; and even, if poffible, during its prefent recefs.

It is not improbable, that, in the courfe of your life, the revolution of human affairs may bring round fome favourable feafon for the radical correction of abufes in our Parliamentary Reprefentation. At that critical conjuncture, great will be the advantage refulting from a previous publication of your Bill; when the then exifting ftate of the country could not have been forefeen, and when no private intereft could be affigned as the motive for your having refumed the fubject. The value of this advantage, perhaps, is not much over-rated, by fuppofing that the poffibility of *your* fuccefs would depend more upon it, than on any other circumftance which can be reafonably imagined.

But

But if the feafon for accomplishing a Reformation of Parliament should be more remote
than I have here fuppofed, yet, whenever it shall
arrive, the worthy Patriots of that day will undoubtedly feel and acknowledge the immenfe
advantage of having had your fyftem laid before
them. To your previous labours, pofterity will
be chiefly indebted for that additional fecurity to
Public Liberty which may be then acquired.
For let us fuppofe Lord Chatham to have formed, and fubmitted to Parliament and to the pub-
iic, the plan which you afterwards propofed:
The confequence would probably have been,
that the diffenfions among the various advocates
of Reformation, to which their late defeat may
be truly imputed, either would not have broken
out, or would have been foon compofed by his
fuperior authority. But if union had been thus
effected, your tafk would have been far lefs arduous than it actually was; and your efforts, in
all human probability, would have been crown-
ed with fuccefs. From the publication of this
Bill by you, fimilar advantages may be expected
hereafter; and, I truft, pofterity will bow to
your authority with equal refpect.*

C 2 　　　　　　　　　But

* At prefent this may appear a hyperbolical compliment;
but when written, it was the honeft expreffion of the Editor's
real fentiments. In the early part of his Adminiftration, much
had been wifely and bravely done by Mr Pitt to repair our fhat-
tered finances, and to reftore œconomy and integrity in the
expenditure of the public money; and it was then expected by
many of his Friends, that to complete our internal fecurity, by
an effectual Reformation of Parliament, would be the grand
object of his political life. He began it as his Father had begun
his, a Foe to Corruption, a Friend to the Rights of the People:
Had

But thefe benefits, to be reaped in a more or lefs diftant futurity, are not the only arguments which recommend the production of your Bill. ‑I think I fee feveral good confequences that would immediately flow from that meafure. If the Bill, with the Schedule annexed, fhould appear next winter, or before the next general election, that advantage might probably be derived from it which I took the liberty to ftate to you, foon after the attempt made by Mr Marfham to disfranchife Queenborough. The idea feemed to meet your entire approbation; but the attack upon that borough not having been renewed, no opportunity has yet occurred to make the propofed experiment. What I mean to fuggeft is this; the magnitude of your plan was, perhaps, in the minds of the major part of your opponents, their principal objection; and yet the very fame perfons who rejected the whole fyftem, may be induced to promote its eftablifhment in detail. For after the next general election, fhould any borough, convicted of corruption, appear to deferve disfranchifement, it is highly probable that by your influence the guilty borough might be punifhed; not, as in the cafes of Shoreham and Cricklade, by imparting the right of voting there to the Freeholders of the Hundred; which is a clumfy regulation, and inapplicable to any great fyf-

---

Had he, like him, perfevered to the end, in his firft attachment to the one, and his hereditary hatred to the other, he would have equalled his father in true glory; he would have furpaffed him, had he with the fame fteadfaftnefs adhered to his original fyftem ot pacific policy, and like Wafhington preferved his country from the calamities of a war with France.

tematical

tematical improvement; but by imparting the juftly-forfeited franchife to thofe great towns and diftricts which are wholly unreprefented, or reprefented with the greateft inadequacy. If this rule of transferring the forfeited franchife fhould then be adopted at your recommendation, it would follow of courfe, that the order of transfers, previoufly publifhed in your Schedule, would alfo be adopted. And after this rule of transfer had taken place in a few inflances, the unfatisfied diftricts contained in the Schedule would acquire a fpecies of right, or equitable claim, that the order of the Schedule fhould continue to be obferved in all future transfers of the right of Reprefentation.—And this would fecure the gradual execution of a principal part of your plan, and would alfo tend directly to promote the accomplifhment of the reft.

In a perfonal view, I am perfuaded that this publication will be advantageous to your character. It will be confidered as a fair and candid proceeding; it will prove that your propofitions had been weighed very maturely; it will exhibit a fyftem of Reprefentation the beft adapted to the ftate of the country and its future fluctuations of property of all which hitherto have been propofed; and, finally, it will leave thofe opponents, who from the mean motives of intereft or refentment, do injuftice to the rectitude of your conduct, no ground whatever, in the whole courfe of this bufinefs, for any plaufible imputation.

It may be objected to the propofed publication of your Bill, that it might, perhaps, afford

occafion

occafion for invidious and malignant reflections.
I fuppofe the objection poffible, without perceiv-
ing its force; but, on the contrary, fhould the
meafure be wholly laid afide, or only delayed till
your retreat from office, or till the return of
great national diftrefs, I conceive in each of
thefe cafes your conduct might be open to cenfure. I am aware that this publication is not
exactly the meafure which fome of your friends
would either recommend or approve; yet, if it
be well calculated to fupport your character with
the public, as I think it is, it would hardly leffen
your weight even with thofe affociates whofe
fentiments on the fubject may be different from
your own.*

But

---

* From the date of this Letter to the month of February
1793, the Editor's correfpondence with Mr Pitt was inter-
rupted, but the connection was yet unbroken. During the
earlier part of this period, the general tenor of his adminiftration continued to meet the Editor's approbation and applaufe.
In the fecure and unfufpecting temper of the nation, then lulled
by Peace, no radical cure for a difordered Conftitution could
be applied with fuccefs, or attempted with prudence. The
groffeft abufes and defects ftill remained in the fyftem of Reprefentation, and their tendency was ftill as pernicious as ever;
but that tendency was checked by the neceffities of the State,
and the influence of popular opinion. The Editor, with the
reft of his countrymen, enjoyed the rifing profperity of England; and was content with them to acquiefce under great
exifting evils, thus mitigated by the œconomical fpirit of the
times, and the prudence of Adminiftration. He trufted that
the rights ftill left to the people were fafe under the protection
of a Patriot Minifter, and that no favourable opportunity would
be loft by Mr Pitt, to fortify and fecure the genuine principles
of the Conftitution.

These flattering hopes were the beft confolation of a few years;
but in the latter part of the period alluded to, the profpect began to change, and a train of meafures, dark and threatening in
their appearance, fhot acrofs the political horizon, and threw a
gloom over the country, which has become deeper and darker
with

But it is time for me to ſtop; I am conſcious my zeal has led me to the edge of impropriety; yet I cannot reſolve to cancel what I have written, becauſe I am alſo conſcious my motives for uſing this freedom are equally right to you and to the public; and therefore, in that view, they are ſure to meet your candid acceptance.

I have only to add, that if you ſhould reſolve to publiſh your Bill, and ſhould wiſh previouſly to ſee me, I will moſt chearfully obey your commands, and come up to London at any time which may beſt ſuit your convenience.

I am, dear Sir,
With very great reſpect and regard,
Your's, moſt faithfully,
C. WYVILL.

with every ſucceeding year. The Editor's ſuſpicions were now renewed with increaſing force; he grew more and more alarmed; he plainly ſaw greater and greater reaſon for it. At laſt, in the beginning of February 1793, the violent ſteps which had been taken, apparently with a deſign to diſgrace and ruin the whole body of Reformers, and engage this country in a raſh and unneceſſary war with France, induced the Editor to addreſs an expoſtulatory Letter to Mr Pitt on theſe ſubjects.

The Letter was privately ſent to him in February 1793; like the two preceding Letters, *it remained unanſwered*, and in the courſe of a few weeks it was publiſhed. Had Mr Pitt deigned to return a ſatisfactory anſwer reſpecting the matters diſcuſſed in it, the Editor's intention was not to publiſh it. But his ſilence, combined with the facts alluded to, appeared, in his judgment, to form a ſtrong preſumptive proof that Mr Pitt had abandoned the liberal and pacific principles of policy which had rendered the early part of his adminiſtration happy and popular, and had adopted a new and dangerous ſyſtem of FOREIGN WAR and INTERNAL COERCION. Under this perſuaſion, Mr Wyvill thought it an indiſpenſible duty to renounce his connection with Mr Pitt, and to lay this expoſtulatory Letter before the public.—It ſeems unneceſſary to republiſh it here.

Paper XVIII.

Extract * *of a* Letter *from the* Rev. C. Wyvill *to* W. Wilberforce, Efq.

Burton-Hall, *March 7th*, 1793.

My dear Sir,

IN my intercourfe with Mr Pitt, many things were imparted to me confidentially, and in no circumftances whatever fhall I think myfelf authorized to divulge any part of thefe communications, without his previous confent. But whatever at any time has been communicated to me refpecting the public bufinefs of the Affociation, by Mr Pitt, by Lord Lanfdown, or by Lord Rockingham, I have not thought fuch communications from men in their minifterial ftations, whether made in writing or in converfation, were private communications to me individually (when fecrecy was not at that time enjoined), ' but as communications of a public nature, made to me in my official capacity, as Chairman of the Yorkfhire Committee. Of fuch communications, in all cafes, whether made in writing or in converfation, I held myfelf bound to give an

* This Extract is placed in the feries of papers which paffed between Mr Pitt and Mr Wyvill, becaufe, though it is taken from a Letter addreffed to Mr Wilberforce, that Letter was intended to be fhown to Mr Pitt, contained an offer to him, and was actually put into his hands by Mr Wilberforce. This appears from Mr Wilberforce's Letter to Mr Wyvill, dated the 30th of July, 1793; and from the fame Letter it alfo appears, that Mr Pitt returned it to Mr Wilberforce " *with no anfwer*."

account

account to the Committee: Papers thus communicated I confidered as public papers, and myfelf bound in refpect of them to act as the Truftee of the Committee and of the Public. This is the light in which I confidered Lord Lanfdown's Letters * to me about ten years ago: He underftood that I kept them back from the public view at that moment, when their appearance might have been perfonally detrimental to him, and injurious to the Public Caufe; but that I did not engage that they fhould be abfolutely and entirely fuppreffed. With my having kept them back at that time, his Lordfhip has frequently expreffed his fatisfaction; at my not engaging to fupprefs them, I have never heard that he, or any friend of his, has expreffed any difpleafure or difapprobation. In the cafe of Lord Lanfdown, I did not confent that a wanton or malevolent ufe fhould be made of his communications; in the cafe of Mr Pitt, which is nearly

---

* With refpect to the publication of Lord Lanfdown's Letters to the Editor in 1782, he ftates with pleafure that his Lordfhip acknowledged the propriety of Mr Wyvill's conduct; expreffed his approbation of publicity in matters of national importance negociated between a Minifter of State and a Public Body of men, or their confidential Agent; and confidered fuch Agent as refponfible for his conduct to his Conftituents and to the Public. This was the magnanimity of a frank and honourable mind, that fcorned all unneceffary concealment. Confcious of having acted in a moft important ftation, with integrity to the Public, and fidelity to a refpectable Body of men, with whom he had entered into engagements, Lord Lanfdown was too candid and equitable to withhold his approbation, or withdraw his efteem from others, who, in a humble ftation, and with fcanty means, have acted on the fame general views; dealing with equal impartiality the fame meafure to Minifters dead or living, to Statefmen *in* or *out* of power, and in dangerous times endeavouring, like him, with honeft zeal to fupport the principles of our finking Conftitution.

fimilar,

fimilar, I fhall act by fimilar rules; I fhall lay myfelf under the fame reftriction, not wantonly or malevolently to publifh " *the Heads of his Bill,*" or any of *his Letters;* ftill, however, referving to myfelf the right which I think I have to retain them in behalf of the public, and in certain cafes to publifh them; particularly in the cafe alluded to in my Letter to Mr Pitt, and more diftinctly ftated in my laft Letter to yourfelf, viz. on the event of Mr Pitt's death, without having effected a Reform in the Reprefentation, and without having publifhed the fame or a better Plan of Reformation. By acting in this manner, I conceive I fhall do my duty to the public, and yet nothing injurious or juftly difpleafing to Mr Pitt. If he wifhes the papers in queftion to be fuppreffed or returned to him, I wifh to gratify him, provided it can be made fufficiently evident that his claim to the difpofal of thefe papers is a juft claim. I profefs, however, that it feems to me highly improbable, or rather impoffible, that he can fhow any juft claim to the difpofal of *the Letters;* it appears upon the face of them that they are public Letters, and they contain nothing, as I think, which upon examination will be found to alter their quality. But the paper intitled " *Heads of a Bill, &c.*" is fomewhat differently circumftanced; and though I do at prefent conceive it to be properly a communication of a public nature, like *the Letters;* yet if there is any circumftance relating to this paper which fhows that it ought not to be fo confidered, I fhall not hefitate to return it to Mr Pitt, when convinced of my

miftake;

miftake; and I will publicly acknowledge my
error, if into an error I have fallen from inadvertence or forgetfulnefs of any material circumftance refpecting this paper, and ftate the
reafons alfo which may have produced that conviction; and that conviction will be produced,
if Mr Pitt will affert to me, that, when the paper
intitled " *Heads of a Bill, &c.*" was communicated to me, he diftinctly recollects, either that he
laid me under an injunction of perpetual fecrecy
refpecting it, or expreffed to me that it was a
paper which he referved the power to recall
when he faw fit, or fomewhat equivalent, clearly
explained at the time. Under thefe circumftances, I fhall think myfelf authorifed to deliver the
paper in queftion back to Mr Pitt, though I do
not myfelf recollect them. But if nothing of
this import can be alledged by Mr Pitt, I fhall
continue to think that I cannot furrender that
paper without fubjecting myfelf to the imputation of treachery to the public, or, at leaft, of
grofs neglect to promote its true intereft. I beg
leave to trouble you again to fhow this Letter to
Mr Pitt.

I am ever, my dear Sir,
With great regard,
Moft faithfully your's,
C. WYVILL

Paper XIX.

Paper XIX.

Letter *from the* Rev. C. Wyvill *to the* Right
Honourable William Pitt.

Burton-Hall, *Jan. 27th,* 1796.

Sir,

I Do not trouble you with this Letter, from
any doubt refpecting the nature of the correfpondence which paffed between us in the earlier part of our intercourfe. I am fully fatisfied
that the papers alluded to are to be confidered,
like my correfpondence with Lord Lanfdown,
as papers of a public nature ; they were communications on a fubject of great importance to the
community ; they paffed between you, in your
official capacity as a Minifter, or as a Member
of Parliament, and the Agent of the Committee
of Affociation of the County of York ; who
deems himfelf refponfible for his conduct in
thofe political negociations to the Public, and
in a more efpecial manner to that Body of Men
who were his Conftituents, and whofe confidence in him was the principal, if not the only,
motive for thofe communications. This was my
opinion before I addreffed my Letter to you,
dated February 9th, 1793 ; and it was formed
on an anxious recollection of the circumftances
relative to the papers in queftion, and an atten-
tive examination of their contents : and in that
opinion I have been much confirmed, fince the
propofal which I made to you in a Letter to our

common

common Friend, Mr Wilberforce, dated March 7th, 1793. This propofal was relative to the publication or conditional fuppreffion of one of the papers alluded to, intitled, " Heads of a Bill, or Bills, for amending the Reprefentation;" and the Letter containing this propofal, foon after its date, was put into your hand by him, and returned to him by you, without an anfwer. The propofal was in effect an offer to return or fupprefs this paper, if you would declare that you underftood it to have been a communication not of a public, but of a private nature; provided I might be at liberty to ftate this declaration to the public, as my juftification for the furrender of the paper. And I confider your filence upon the occafion of this offer, as a proof that, although you was unwilling to own, you found yourfelf unable to deny, that the paper in queftion is a paper of a public nature, and had been communicated to me under no condition of fecrecy, under no reftriction or referve whatever, expreffed or underftood, at the time of its communication; and that no promife or engagement had been fubfequently made on my part, which could juftly be conftrued to have taken away my right to hold this paper as a truftee for the public, and eventually to publifh it in the cafe of your death, or in the cafe of your hoftility to the caufe of Reform, and your ultimate refufal to produce it.

But from this clear eftablifhment of my right to publifh the paper in queftion in each of thefe cafes, the duty to publifh it immediately is not inferred. In this refpect, I think myfelf war-
ranted

ranted to affume a certain latitude, or difcre-
tionary power of delay; and you, Sir, on this
occafion, may with reafon expect from me every
mark of attention which is reconcilable with my
duty to the public. I fhould be extremely forry
to produce this paper to general infpection, if
you really mean to publifh it in its prefent
form, or improved with fuch corrections, as the
experience of more than ten years in the higheft
official fituation may have fuggefted to you.
And yet it is poffible that you meditate no corrections, that you intend to publifh the Heads
of your Bill neither in their prefent ftate, nor in
any improved ftate; it is poffible that you may
have changed your political opinions, that you
may wifh to confign the paper in queftion to
oblivion, with every other memorial of thofe
tranfactions for effecting a Reform of Parliament, in which you bore the principal part.
But I ftill continue to think, as I thought in the
earlier period of our connection, that a fubftantial, moderate, and timely Reformation of Parliament, is neceffary for the prefervation of our
National Liberty. For this purpofe, I confider the Heads of your Bill of Reform as an
important paper, which I hold in truft for the
public; and therefore I could not innocently
concur with you to conceal it, if fuch fhould be
your defign; it even feems incumbent upon me
to take effectual meafures to fecure the publication of it, by you or by myfelf.

I do not affert that you wifh to withhold the
paper in queftion from the public eye; but I
think that, under the various circumftances of
the

the cafe, recent and remote, it would be fimpli-
city, it would be folly and credulity in any man
to believe that your political fyftem remains as
favourable to popular rights as it was in the
year 1785. In me it would be the weaknefs of
idiocy, after having witneffed the four laft years
of your adminiftration, and waited ten years for
the production of this paper by yourfelf, ftill to
confide, ftill to acquiefce, ftill to wait on, in
filent expectation of its appearance; forgetting
the uncertainty of life, the approaching infirmi-
ties of age, and foolifhly declining to interpofe
in behalf of the public, till any interpofition on
my part might be no longer in my power. From
thefe confiderations, I am convinced that I ought
not to delay explicitly to open my mind to you,
and endeavour to obtain a diftinct declaration of
your intentions.

I do therefore avow my fufpicion of your hoftility to the caufe of Political Reformation, and
of your purpofe never to publifh the paper in
queftion.

The tafk which this avowal of my diftruft
compels me to undertake, I feel is a painful one.
But it would be falfehood and bafe flattery to
difclaim my fufpicion; it would be defpicable
diffimulation to act as if confidence were entire,
and precaution unneceffary; and it would be
treachery to the public, to neglect the employ-
ment of thofe obvious means which are within
my reach, and by which the production of the
document in queftion by yourfelf may be fecured, or its publication by me may be proved
to

to have been a neceſſary act of juſtice to the country.

Feeling theſe impreſſions ,on my mind, I am not deterred by the unfavourable circumſtance of your having returned no anſwer to the former propoſal, from offering to you one propoſition more ; and I now offer it with the ſincerity of a heart which is unconſcious of any inducement but the anxious wiſh to aſcertain and perform my duty to the public, and as far, as may be conſiſtent with that duty, to avoid doing what may be unacceptable to you.—My offer is briefly this, that if you will have the goodneſs to declare, that you intend to publiſh the Heads of your Bill for reforming the Repreſentation in their preſent ſtate, or improved by ſuch cor-rections as your experience may have ſuggeſted, I ſhall moſt willingly acquieſce, and lay aſide my deſign to publiſh that paper. But I muſt be underſtood to be at liberty to repreſent this circumſtance as my reaſon for omitting that piece in the 4th volume of Political Papers which I am now preparing for the preſs; and I muſt alſo be conſidered as ſtill holding that paper in truſt for the public.

It is the verſatility of the Stateſman which I diſtruſt, and appearances may probably be thought to juſtify the ſuſpicion ; yet I ſtill re-ſpect, and would rely on, the perſonal honour and integrity of the Man. And as I will not deny that appearances, however ſtrong they may have been, poſſibly may have deceived and a-larmed me too much ; ſo you, I think, cannot

juſtly

juftly alledge that my fufpicion has been formed on flight and frivolous grounds, or avowed with unfriendly hafte, and in an indecorous tone. If then you really mean to publifh your Plan, and in truth you ftill continue a friend to moderate Reformation, can there be any good reafon why fo natural a mifconception fhould not be rectified? In fuch a cafe, furely, condefcention on your part, to remove miftaken fears, and to fatisfy honeft fcruples, could be no dishonour; as on mine, I truft, acquiefcence on the conditions propofed could be no breach of duty to the public.

But if you fhould deem it expedient to return no anfwer to this offer, or fhould anfwer it in a manner that comes not up to the terms propofed, I fhall not hefitate to draw the obvious conclufion from your filence. In that cafe, I fhall proceed, as it may fuit my convenience, to publifh the paper in queftion, with the other papers not included in this offer, which paffed between us in the courfe of our correfpondence.*　　I am, Sir,

　　　　Your moft obedient humble fervant,
　　　　　　　C. WYVILL.

　D　　　　　　　Paper XX.

---

* This Letter was fent to Mr Pitt, by the poft, on the day of its date; and in a fhort time after that, a Duplicate, in which two or three verbal corrections were made, was fent to James Martin, Efq. the worthy Member for Tewkfbury; by whom it was delivered into Mr Pitt's hands, in the Houfe of Commons, on the 17th of February, 1796. For this kind affiftance, Mr Wyvill returns Mr Martin his moft fincere and grateful acknowledgments; happy to owe fo important a fervice to a friend equally diftinguifhed for his candour, benevolence, and
all

Paper XX.

The Cafe *of the* Rev. C. WYVILL *refpecting the* Right Honourable WILLIAM PITT, *and his* Paper, *intituled,* " Heads of a Bill or Bills for amending the Reprefentation."

BURTON-HALL, *April 6th,* 1796.

IT has always been the writer's wifh to pafs his life in the peace and privacy of a country retirement. It has been his good fortune, and he is thankful for it, to have fpent the largeft and beft portion of his days, fince he attained to manhood, in this moft pleafant retreat. For the laft twenty-two years, he has been an inhabitant of Yorkfhire; and during the far greateft part of this period, he has enjoyed domeftic peace and happinefs in retirement and wedded fociety, with this added fatisfaction during the latter part of this period, that much of his attention, and many of his hours, have been employed in the pleafing cares of educating his numerous family of children, and providing for their intereft and future welfare.

During this confiderable fpace of time, amufement has feldom induced him to refort to the crowded haunts of men. Privacy he has preferred, becaufe privacy was more agreeable to his

all the milder virtues of private life; and for his firmnefs and intrepidity in the Senate, as a defender of the rights of his fellow-citizens, and a friend to the true intereft of his country.

Of the Duplicate alluded to, the Letter printed here is a copy.—At the time of its publication, *no anfwer* had been received from Mr Pitt.

tafte.

taſte. He was pleaſed with the blamelefs occu-
pations, the innocent amuſements, of a country
life ; he loved the contemplation of nature, and
viewed with delight the beauties of the change-
ful feaſons, and the leſs varying, yet not wholly
fixed and ſtationary, beauties of the ſcenes a-
round him. But retirement was his choice for
reafons of greater weight and gravity. He valued his independence ; he felt the honeſt pride
of a freeman ; and independence and freedom
he knew were beſt preſerved at a diſtance from
the prodigality and enſnaring allurements of the
capital. He is far, very far, from being as virtuous as he ought, and as he ſincerely wiſhes to
be ; yet, though not extremely virtuous, he is a
lover of virtue, and though not profoundly learned, he is a friend to learning ; and, in his opinion, the cultivation of virtue, and the purſuits
of literature, are uſually moſt ſuccefsful in retirement. There might be in his temper ſome al-
loy of indolence and diffidence, which inclined
him to a ſequeſtered life : But even his adverſa-
ries are abundantly ready to teſtify, that, on various public occaſions, he has not been ſlow to
ſtand forth, nor afraid to act his part in the buſy
ſcene of politics. He adds, what they will be
leſs willing to acknowledge, that he has never
engaged in political buſineſs, but from a ſenſe of
duty to his country ; from a deteſtation of corruption, that execrable principle of Government ;
from indignation at direct and open invaſions of
our rights ; and from an honeſt zeal to defend
public liberty, oppreſſed and endangered by an
Adminiſtration once friendly to popular rights

D 2   —after

—after that, fternly fevere and refolute to deftroy them.—The ends he aimed at, were the
reftoration of national morals, then finking under the debafing influence of our Government;
and the prefervation of our Conftitution on
its genuine principles, then nearly defaced by
the wear of pafling ages, and almoft loft under
the immenfe accumulation of abufes. The ends
were good and laudable; the means were unexceptionable, and becoming the ends: Argumen-
tation at legal affemblies of the people, petitions,
remonftrances, affociations, engagements to vote
againft corruption and corrupt men,—thefe were
the means to attain his objects; thefe were the
weapons of his political warfare; the only weapons he will ever employ; convinced that virtuous men, united for the defence of liberty, by
reafon alone, muft ultimately fucceed againft all
oppofition: And hence, in any event, they will
be fure to derive the beft reward of their labours, that perfect fatisfaction of mind, that con-
fcioufnefs of unimpeachable virtue, which no
rafh appeal to force can ever beftow.

But though it has been his happy lot to lead
a great part of his life in privacy and in the
country, yet, on the occafions alluded to, he
has feen enough of the world of politics to be
fully convinced, that neither probity, nor any
prudential caution, can fecure the opponent of
national abufes againft the rancorous tooth of
calumny. He has feen this in the cafe of men
much better than himfelf; he has felt it in his
own. He knows there are bigots in politics,
as in religion; in both he is aware that the

rage

rage of paffionate men, and the malice of cooler men, interefted in the prefervation of abufes, ever will purfue the beft-intentioned promoters of Reformation. He, therefore, expects no exemption from their injurious attacks; but, trufting in the fhield of integrity, he is prepared to meet his adverfaries with fortitude, and to bear their flanders with patience. Though he reverence the judgment of the public, he has feldom troubled it with the refutation of calumnies. To any vague imputations of fedition or treafon; to any anonymous falfehood, charging him with the guilt of a regicide and a traitor to his country, no reply in future, he trufts, will be neceffary: He will leave accufations fo wholly deftitute of foundation to fall of themfelves, as they foon muft, down to the ground. Indeed, by fome attacks, it would be folly to be provoked or difcouraged. The infects which have long been endeavouring to annoy him, bear the hornet's fpite in their hearts, and an acrid venom in their tails; but their fting is too feeble to inject it. He would not crufh the tirefome creatures; he would only fhun them. Does this language found too contemptuous? He fincerely pities the perfons alluded to; but he cannot think of their conduct to him, without fome mixture of contempt.

Widely different are the fenfations which have been produced in his mind by the cenfure of men, for whom he has been long accuftomed to feel the warmeft affection, and the fincerity of whofe friendfhip to him he cannot queftion. He willingly admits their general candour; he high-

ly

ly efteems their various talents; but he denies
the juftice of their reprehenfion refpecting his
behaviour to Mr Pitt. In this refpect, they have
condemed *his paft* and *his intended* conduct; his
allufion to the " Heads " of Mr Pitt's Bill, in the
printed Letter to him of February 1793, and
his declared intention to publifh that paper in
the event of Mr Pitt's death, or in the contingency of his hoftility to the caufe of Reformation, and his ultimate refufal to publifh it
himfelf.

He trufts, however, he fhall be able to imprefs on an impartial public the fame conviction
which he feels himfelf, viz. that, in the cafes alluded to, his conduct has been, and will be,
perfectly confiftent with the ftricteft and moft
correct morality. But if his plea fhould fail to
produce the fame conviction on the minds of
thofe friends whofe hafty difapprobation he wifhes to remove, he will lament his misfortune, and
impute it to no perfonal unkindnefs, to no defi-
ciency in general candour and equity, but to
the warmth of an early friendfhip for the Minifter, or the ftill more fafcinating effect of an en-
thufiaftic admiration of his genius and character.
The bias thus hung upon the mind may be unperceived, but its power to miflead the judgment
may be ftrong and nearly irrefiftible.

The juftification of Mr Wyvill's paft conduct,
in alluding to the " Heads," will be found to reft
on the following facts and obfervations : The
force of the obfervations may be varioufly felt;
the facts, he trufts, will be undifputed by Mr
Pitt, or his moft partial friends.

1. Mr

ɪ. Mr Wyvill afferts, that the intercourfe between Mr Pitt and him was an intercourfe not
of private friendfhip and perfonal attachment,
but of political connection on public grounds.
His acquaintance with Mr Pitt, as he recollects,
commenced in the fpring of the year 1780. Mr
Pitt was, at that time, a very young man, and
had not made his appearance in Parliament. Mr
Wyvil! was then attending a Meeting of Deputies, appointed to prepare a plan of National Affociation, for effecting a Reformation of Parliament. He was one of the three Gentlemen de-
legated by the County of York for that purpofe.
Vifcount Mahon was deputed by the County of
Kent to attend the fame Meeting. The tranfac-
tion of the bufinefs for which they had been deputed, neceffarily required frequent communication between the Deputies: Lord Mahon and Mr
Wyvill foon found that they were agreed in their
hatred to a corrupt fyftem of Adminiftration; in
their zealous attachment to Liberty, on the genuine principles of the Conftitution; and in their
firm conviction, that, without a radical reform
of abufes in the frame of Parliament itfelf, the
official regulations propofed by Burke, as the
grand panacea for all our national complaints,
would be found no better than trifling altera-
tives, or tranfient anodynes, whofe flight and infignificant effect would foon be overpowered by
the deeply-vitiated habit of our Reprefentative
Body. They feared that by a falfe complaifance
in the Meeting of Deputies to the Agent of the
old Ariftocracy, the opportunity to effect a moderate Reform in the Houfe of Commons might

be

be unwifely loft, and thus the nation would be left expofed to the danger, either of an affumption of Defpotic Power on the one hand, or the calamities of a violent Revolution on the other hand; and they were perfectly agreed in their wifhes and endeavours to prevent this fatal overfight in the popular counfels at that time.—This general fimilarity in their principles and views, produced an intimacy between the noble Vifcount and the writer, which gradually became confidential, and which the eventful feries of fixteen years has not diminifhed, he trufts, on either fide. To his truly noble Friend, Mr Wyvill owed his introduction to Mr Pitt's acquaintance : It was at Lord Mahon's houfe that he was firft made known to Mr Pitt; but whether the introduction was propofed by Lord Mahon, or defired by Mr Pitt, he does not diftinctly recollect.—At this interview, the fentiments of Mr Pitt, on the dangerous fituation of the country at that time, on the corrupt ftate of Parliament, and the neceffity for its Reformation at the requeft and interpofition of the people, were fimilar to thofe of Lord Mahon and the other Member of the General Deputation. This, at leaft, was then, and ever fince has been, the opinion of Mr Wyvill. To fufpect the fincerity of Mr Pitt at that time, muft be groundlefs and injurious jealoufy. He had been bred at the feet of Gamaliel, in the ftricteft principles of the Conftitution; he had been imbued by his father with his own ardent love of liberty, his own fcorn of corruption, and his ftrong defire for a purer ftrain of Government under the con-

trouling

trouling influence of a Reformed Reprefentation. It feems impoffible to fuppofe, that doc-
trines fo congenial to the purity and generous
zeal of a youthful mind, recommended by fuch
a Preceptor, and that Preceptor his Father, were
not embraced by Mr Pitt with fincerity and ardour. When he heard corruption avowed without fhame, and faw it practifed with impunity;
when the corrupt prodigality of Minifters increafed with the public difapprobation of their
meafures, and their mifconduct had driven the
country to the brink of ruin, it was natural, and
nearly unavoidable, that the Son of Chatham
fhould be indignant at the fight, and fhould de-
vote his utmoft efforts to extirpate this deep-
rooted evil, this baneful corruption, from our
Parliamentary Syftem.

But for fome years after this introduction,
their general concurrence in thefe political fentiments produced little intercourfe between Mr
Pitt and Mr Wyvill, chiefly for want of opportunity on the part of Mr Wyvill to cultivate an
acquaintance he fo highly valued. On Mr
Pitt's firft motion in Parliament on the fubject
of Reformation,* Mr Wyvill had not the honour
of any communication with Mr Pitt. After
the rejection of that motion, they both attended
a public Meeting at the Thatched Houfe,† when
the refolution propofed by Mr Wyvill, with a
view to animate the nation to fupport the intended exertions of Mr Pitt in the fucceeding
Seffion, appeared to meet his entire approbation.

---

* On the 7th of May, 1782.

† On the 18th of May, 1782.   Before

Before that Seffion commenced, Mr Pitt had entered the Cabinet. His introduction there, added new weight to his recommendation; the declaration of intended support by Lord Shelburne, then principal Minister, was still more encouraging; Yorkshire and many other Districts petitioned for Reform; and on the 7th of May, 1783, Mr Pitt proposed to Parliament resolutions nearly coincident with those propositions which had been adopted by the Affociation of Yorkshire. On this occasion, Mr Wyvill had the honour of a conference with Mr Pitt; and this interview gradually produced more and more intimate communications. After the defeat of the India Bill in the next Seffion, Mr Pitt succeeded the Duke of Portland in the station of principal Minister: His efforts for Reform, though unfuccefsful, had won him much and deferved popularity; and to that popularity he owed his elevation. In the recent struggle on the India Bill, his friends in Yorkshire had applauded his conduct; and when the House of Commons endeavoured to embarrafs the meafures of the new Minister, they fupported him with vigour at a County Meeting. This was an effential fervice, which contributed in a confiderable degree to fix in his favour the then fluctuating opinion of the public. As foon, therefore, as he found himfelf a little better fecured in the poffeffion of his power, he refolved to gratify his northern friends, and to make another effort, with all his might, to accomplifh their favourite meafure. On this occafion he changed his ground, and his mode of procedure; and inftead of moving for a Committee

mittee of Inquiry, as in 1782, or offering fome fpecific Refolutions, as in 1783, he propofed his new and more-extended meafure in the fhape of a Bill. The County of York, at a Meeting held fome time before, had adopted certain propofitions as an amendment to their Affociation. The principles laid down by Mr Pitt in his fpeech to Parliament on the 18th of April, 1785, were correfpondent with thofe propofitions ; but his judgment had fuggefted various improvements, which his fuperior fkill worked up, and formed a plan of Reformation at once the moft extenfive and effectual, and at the fame time the moft mild and practicable, which had been devifed.

Soon after this generous refolution had been fixed by Mr Pitt, he communicated his intention to Mr Wyvill; the intercourfe between them became more frequent and intimate ; and Mr Wyvill had the honour to be confulted in the progrefs of the bufinefs, with refpect to the mode of obtaining moft effectually the popular fupport to the intended motion, and alfo with refpect to various modifications and corrections of the Plan. After the rejection of the motion by Parliament in 1785, the fame perfonal intercourfe continued for fome time; till at laft, in 1787, the nation had become indifferent to all queftions of Reform, and the hope of fuccefs, in that temper of the public, was quite extinguifhed.—After this period, Mr Wyvill ceafed to hold any perfonal intercourfe with Mr Pitt ; but their political connection remained unbroken till the beginning of 1793. It had been commenced in 1780, from a fimilarity of political opinion ; it became intimate

mate and unreferved during Mr Pitt's ftruggle
to effect a Reformation of Parliament; and it
ceafed when his hoftility to his own former meafures appeared to Mr Wyvill, in 1793, to be no
longer queftionable. It is true, that during this
connection much perfonal efteem and attachment to Mr Pitt were mixed with the political
confidence which Mr Wyvill felt and profeffed:
But in 1783, and the three fubfequent years,
the intercourfe between them was not that of
private friends, but that of a great Statefman
treating with a very humble individual, the confidential Agent of a body of men, whofe propofitions of Reform he had refolved to adopt, and
whofe political fupport he wifhed to obtain: And
therefore, in Mr Wyvill's conception, communications on the public bufinefs of his conftituents are not to be confidered by fuch Agent
as trufts of a private and confidential nature,
but are properly to be underftood as public
communications, unlefs it were otherwife expreffed at the time when fuch communications were
made.

2. Mr Wyvill afferts, that the Letters and
other Papers of Mr Pitt, particularly the " *Heads
of a Bill, or Bills, for amending the Reprefentation,*" were imparted by him to Mr Wyvill
under no feal of fecrecy, under no particular
reftriction or limitation expreffed or underftood
at the time, and that no fubfequent promife or
engagement was entered into by Mr Wyvill,
which in any juft or rational conftruction can
be confidered as binding him to furrender the
Paper in queftion to Mr Pitt, or to fupprefs it,

or during his life not to publifh it. It is far
from his intention to conceal that, refpecting the
Heads of Mr Pitt's Bill, a certain promife was
made by Mr Wyvill, which he confiders himfelf
to have fulfilled literally, and alfo in its fpirit
and moft extenfive meaning. This fhall be explained with fidelity, and with all the brevity
which may be confiftent with clearnefs and pre-
cifion.—Immediately, or very foon after the rejection of Mr Pitt's motion on the 18th of April,
for amending the Reprefentation, Mr Wyvill
waited upon him, and propofed that this Bill
might be drawn and publifhed without delay.
Among other reafons for the meafure, which are
alluded to in the Letter of the 29th of July,
1787, this alfo, as Mr Wyvill believes, was fuggefted to Mr Pitt, viz. that when the alterations
propofed had been diftinctly ftated and laid before the public in the ufual form of a Bill, publifhed by himfelf, Meetings of the Friends of Political Reformation might be held, by whom the
Plan thus authenticated might be confidered and
approved ; and thus the hitherto disjointed Party
of Reformers might be united in one firm and
compact Body, by whofe unanimous efforts the
fuccefs of Mr Pitt's exertions, in the next Seffion,
or at leaft in the courfe of the exifting Parliament, might moft probably be fecured. To this
fuggeftion, Mr Pitt objected the impoffibility of
complying with it during this Seffion, on account
of the preffure of public bufinefs, and the formidable oppofition in Parliament. He wifhed to
referve the Bill till the favourable moment for
carrying it was arrived, and in the mean time to
avail

avail himfelf of all the light which could be thrown upon the fubject, in order that every objection might be more maturely confidered, every difficulty might be more effectually obviated, and every correction and improvement might be introduced, which would meliorate his Plan, and render it at once acceptable to Parliament and the Public.

Soon after this interview with Mr Pitt, Mr Wyvill was honoured with another, which he requefted at the defire of a previous Meeting of Gentlemen, friendly to his moderate propofal of Reformation, and anxious to unite the various bands of Reformers on this ground. Their refolution requefting an authentic copy of his Plan was communicated to Mr Pitt: It was fuggefted to him, that although, for the reafons lately ftated, it might be expedient to poftpone the publication of his Bill for fome time; yet another method might be taken, if it fhould meet his approbation, which would anfwer the purpofe for which the Gentlemen had folicited a copy of his Plan: That method was, to fubftitute a Summary Explanation of the Principles of his Bill, inftead of the Bill itfelf, to be drawn by Mr Wyvill, but authenticated to the intended Meeting by Mr Pitt. This would afford the proper ground for paffing refolutions of thanks and approbation; and thus the various fects and fubdivifions of the Reformers might be induced to coalefce and fupport his plan with their united ftrength. Of this idea Mr Pitt exprefled his approbation, provided care were taken in drawing the Summary Explanation, abfolutely to avoid
every

every allufion to the *Heads of his Bill for amending the Reprefentation*. The reafon for this re-
ftri&ion, as Mr Wyvill recolle&s, was this;
that any fuch allufion would afford an opportunity to fome of his acute and vigilant opponents in the Houfe of Commons to call upon
him for the publication of the Bill itfelf; a
call with which, for the reafons he had given, it
would at that time be extremely inconvenient to
comply, and yet with which compliance could
not be refufed, without hurting his chara&er in
the opinion of his reforming friends. With this
reftri&ion Mr Wyvill promifed that his Explanation fhould be exa&ly conformable: It was
drawn accordingly, with no reference to the
" *Heads ;*" it was feen and approved by Mr
Pitt, and laid before the Meeting at the Thatch-
ed-Houfe on the 24th of May, 1785; with authority from Mr Pitt to declare to the Meeting, that
he acknowledged the Explanation to contain an
exa& and accurate account of the Principles of
his intended Bill for amending the Reprefentation. This was the literal performance of the
only promife or engagement made by Mr Wyvill
refpe&ing the Paper in queftion ; and his filence
upon this fubje& till the year 1793, amounts, in
his conception, to the fulleft performance of it
in fpirit and in meaning. A promife not to
allude to a certain Paper, upon a particular
occafion, and for particular reafons mentioned
at the time when the promife is required, is not
equivalent to a promife of perpetual fecrecy; nor
can it be confidered as binding on a change of
circumftances, under which thofe reafons have
plainly

plainly ceafed to exift. In the year 1785, the Minifter's power refted on no ftable or fecure foundation; the Ariftocracy, reinforced by the perfonal friends, and led by the fuper-eminent genius, of Mr Fox, prefented to Mr Pitt a formidable phalanx of opponents, and the Crown viewed him with fear and jealoufy, which nothing, could have overcome but the fuperior dread of his Great Rival. In this arduous and critical fituation, Mr Pitt feared to call forth the animadverfions of his adverfaries on the fubject of Reform, for they might prove extremely embarraffing; and he wifhed not to excite the fufpicions of his earlieft and moft fincere friends, for their fupport could not then be fpared. But in 1793, the circumftances of his political fituation were advantageoufly changed: The confidence of the Crown was won; the ftrength of his Rival was weakened by defertions; the great Body of the Ariftocracy was united with him, and his exorbitant power feemed fixed on a folid and permanent foundation: From the oppofition of his Antagonift, he had nothing to fear; from the affiftance of his Reforming Friends, he had nothing to hope. Thus circumftanced, he did not fcruple to give his negative, in a lefs peremptory tone at firft, to Mr Flood's propofition of Reform in the year 1790; and in 1792, he oppofed, with an appearance of more confirmed hoftility, an intimation of a fimilar motion by Mr Grey, and the motion itfelf in 1793. From this conduct it feems rightly to be collected, that the reafons no longer exifted for which filence had been required and promifed; and, therefore,

that

that Mr Wyvill's engagement had been completely fulfilled in fpirit, as well as in the letter of it, by his filence down to the year 1793. The juftice of this conclufion will be farther confirmed by the confideration, that filence was required by Mr Pitt, not merely to prevent embarraffment to himfelf, but alfo for other more important reafons. In 1785 he was undoubtedly a zealous friend to the Reformation of Parliament; honour and intereft concurred with his early prejudices to infpire that zeal; they pointed to that line of conduct as the road at once to power and true glory. When he delivered the Heads of his Bill to Mr Wyvill, the Paper was unaccompanied with any condition or referve whatever. To determine with what intention it was thus delivered, it muft be confidered what were his principles, what were his views at that time: Thefe, it has been feen, were decidedly favourable to the caufe of Reformation; and hence the conclufion follows undeniably, that the Paper in queftion was put into Mr Wyvill's hands with a view to promote the caufe of Reformation. Within two months after this Paper had been thus committed to Mr Wyvill's cuftody, in truft for the public, Mr Pitt required fecrecy refpecting it, on a particular occafion, for public as well as private reafons, which have been already ftated, exactly conformable with that view which at firft induced him to deliver it to Mr Wyvill. The referve was neceffary, to prevent inconvenience to himfelf; it was neceffary alfo, to prevent injury to the common caufe. The perfonal inconvenience was

E

a circumſtance of tranſient duration; and reſpecting it, the writer's obligation to ſilence
ſeems to have been fulfilled in 1793. He, therefore, conſidered himſelf as then free from that
engagement, and under the ſole obligation, in
conformity with the truſt originally repoſed in
him, to conſult the intereſt of the cauſe of Reformation. The leaſt extended idea of that truſt
bound him, he thought, to hold " *The Heads* "
in behalf of the public, and in the contingent
events of Mr Pitt's death, or his abſolute hoſtility
to Reform, to lay that Paper before the public.

In the event of Mr Pitt's death, the obligation
to publiſh the Heads ſeems inconteſtible; and
by parity of reaſon, in the event of his manifeſt
hoſtility to Reform, the ſame obligation ſeems
equally well founded. For let it be ſuppoſed,
that from a change of intereſt or opinio., the
ardour of Mr Pitt to defend the rights of the
people is cooled, that his patriotic ſpirit is damp-
ed and extinguiſhed by the mephitic gas of the
Houſe of Commons, that his feelings are dead
to the cauſe of Reformation, and alive only to
the ſupport of that ſyſtem which he had ſolemn-
ly engaged to deſtroy: In theſe circumſtances, it
is evident that the publication in queſtion would
be more neceſſary than it would have been even
in the contingency of the Miniſter's death. If
that event had happened a few years ago, it
would have deprived the cauſe of Reformation
of its ableſt and moſt powerful advocate: By his
hoſtility to that cauſe, the Reformers not only
loſe their Leader, but they find his abilities turned againſt them; aided by the impoſing credit
which

which his former zeal had procured him—rein-forced by the formidable power of that ſtation to which their confidence had contributed to raiſe him. To aſcertain that hoſtility with pre-ciſion, may be a taſk as difficult as it muſt be painful to the Truſtee; but from the faƈt once clearly eſtabliſhed, his obligation to publiſh re-ſults with equal certainty in this caſe as in the other, and the neceſſity for it is more indiſpen-ſible. Such in 1793 were his conceptions of the nature of the truſt repoſed in him, and ſuch his ideas of the duty which future circumſtances might call him to perform.

At that time the tenor of Mr Pitt's conduƈt for ſome years had excited ſtrong ſuſpicions in his mind, that the public principles of the Mi-niſter were changed, that he was become hoſtile to Reformation, and never would publiſh his Bill. He felt it to be his duty, if time ſhould prove theſe ſuſpicions to be juſt, neither to con-cur with Mr Pitt in his tergiverſation, nor in compliance with his new ſyſtem to ſuppreſs the Paper in queſtion; but in conformity with his intentions when that Paper was communicated, to execute his truſt with fidelity to the public. In purſuance of theſe ideas, the alluſion to the " Heads " was publiſhed in 1793; it was an in-timation to Mr Pitt, but leſs diſtinƈt and explicit than a ſubſequent intimation, that his ſincerity was ſuſpeƈted; and it was a notification to him, that, *in certain conceivable circumſtances,* Mr Wy-vill held himſelf bound to publiſh this Paper.

From theſe plain faƈts and obſervations, he truſts, it will be the deciſion of his candid and

E 2   im-

impartial judges, that the allufion in 1793 to the "Heads" of Mr Pitt's Bill was an innocent and juftifiable action. On the fame grounds it may be admitted alfo, that he has a right to hold that Paper in truft for the public, and to publifh it in the event of Mr Pitt's death; and even before that event, in the cafe of his manifeft hoftility to the caufe of Reformation. That right he may be allowed to poffefs; but to exercife it upon flight prefumptions, conjectural furmifes, or even plaufible probabilities of Mr Pitt's tergiverfation, this, it may be faid, would be invidious and unbecoming; and if not a breach of truft, would at leaft be a very indifcreet, or a very malevolent, abufe of it. And here it is readily granted, that the publication of that Paper without the Donor's confent, on a hafty and flightly founded fuppofition of hoftility, would be reprehenfible conduct in the Truftee; but he contends, that, on a rapid review of the whole cafe, the proofs will be found completely fatisfactory; fuch as a man of candour will affent to—fuch as a man of probity ought to act on; and to which no additional ftrength of evidence could well be given, but by a direct avowal of hoftility from the Minifter himfelf; for which the Truftee furely cannot be expected to wait.

1. From the rejection of Mr Pitt's motion of Reform in 1785, to the prefent moment, is a period of nearly eleven years. During this long courfe of time, Mr Pitt has not found a proper opportunity to publifh his Bill, or to bring forward his motion of Reform afrefh; and to the propofitions which other Reformers have advanced,

ced, at different times, he has given his uniform oppofition. To juftify his inactivity in the former part of this period, it may be truly alledged, that the public was become too languid in the purfuit of Reformation to afford a profpect of fuccefs; to excufe it in the latter part, it may be pretended, that the great mafs of the people were become fo zealous for Reform, and had adopted fuch extenfive expectations of change, that any attempt to innovate would be dangerous. But the tranfitions of popular opinion are not like thofe of the weather, fudden and momentary; the paffage of the nation from cold to hot, from too little zeal to too much, was undoubtedly gradual; and in this progrefs of opinion, there muft have been a time when the nation had reached that happy temperature of zeal, without excefs, when moderate Reform might have been propofed with fafety, and with a fair probability of fuccefs. Why was not this attempted by the Minifter in the year 1790, or in 1791? Surely not becaufe there was then too much zeal for change; for a contrary reafon was oppofed to Mr Flood. And why did he difcourage Reform in the two fucceeding years? Surely not becaufe there was too little zeal for Reformation; for a contrary reafon was oppofed to Mr Grey. Mr Pitt is too fagacious to have overlooked the golden opportunity; the juft conclufion is, his fyftem was changed.

2. With this conclufion his other meafures about this time accord, and confirm the fuppofition. The Proclamations againft Sedition were drawn in terms of fuch extenfive import, as

E 3   would

would have condemned himself and his own former meafures, had a fimilar edict been iffued in the year 1782. The profeffed object of thefe Proclamations was, to ftigmatize and difgrace the rafh Republican, who had then dared to libel the Conftitution of England; and his deluded followers, who aimed with him not to repair, but to overthrow the fabric of our Government. But by the infidious terms in which thofe Proclamations were drawn, the former friends of the Minifter were comprehended in the common mafs of feditious delinquents, and the peaceful adherents of his own moderate plan of Reformation were injurioufly claffed with men who fought the eftablifhment of a democratic Government through all the calamities of a civil war and a forcible Revolution.

3. After having thus difgraced the caufe of moderate Reform in the eyes of the public, and expofed his earlieft friends to the malice of informers and the rage of political bigots, he has purfued the lefs cautious Reformers in every part of the kingdom with unrelenting feverity; the conviction of fome of thefe unfortunate perfons has been effected in a mode difgraceful to the Judicature of our country, and the punifhment inflicted upon others has been fuch as humanity cannot but lament and difapprove. Of fome of thefe patriot criminals the only guilt has been, that they prefumed to exprefs, in language once the Minifter's, their contempt and deteftation of public abufes: of others the crime proved has been, that, following his example, they have dared to animate and exhort the people in their feveral

counties

counties and districts to meet, to associate, and to exert every legal power then vested in the collective body to destroy those abuses, and restore the Legislature to its ancient purity. For offences like these, they have been tried as incendiaries and felons; they have been doomed to long imprisonment, or a worse transportation to a savage land. After that, the rancour of official prosecution charged some of the most distinguished of these Reformers with the guilt of Treason. A part of them were tried and absolved by their country; but ministerial petulance dared to condemn them. At last the Juries, by their unshaken adherence to justice, discouraged the odious pursuit; and the rest of these victims were dismissed without a trial, to repair their health and fortunes, shattered and broken by the rigours of confinement, and to enjoy their innocence as well as they could in the bosom of their ruined families. Some of those persons might be rash and misguided zealots, who advanced inadmissible claims of Reform, and promoted those claims by means which no friend to peace and order will undertake to justify. Universal suffrage seems to be unadvisable in the present corrupt state of society: extremely numerous assemblies of the people always have some tendency to disorder and tumult; and in any state of society, disorder and tumult ought to be checked and repressed. But to a Government supported as our's is, by an immense revenue, and the greatest military force ever maintained in Britain, a few rash men could not be justly formidable. To the Minister of Reform

E 4   they

they were objects not of his vindictive purfuit,
but of his lenity and forbearance; for his example had mifled them. Inftead, therefore, of ex-
aggerating their indifcretions into acts of Treafon, it would have well become him to have
pardoned them; mixing with his mercy due vi-
gilance to prevent any dangerous exceffes, and
haftening to clofe the fource of difcontent and
difturbance, by granting a prudent redrefs of
thofe grievances, of which, he cannot deny, they
juftly complain.

4. But inftead of redrefs, the Minifter gave the
people a war; furious, bloody, and portending
incalculable evils to England. The origin of this
great calamity may be traced with probability to
a concurrence of circumftances apparently fortuitous and infignificant. It chanced, or, to fpeak
more properly, it was permitted by Providence,
that, during the tempefts of the French Revolution, two very extraordinary men, Thomas Paine
and Edmund Burke, fhould appear in this country: Each of thefe perfonages is endowed with
that fanatical zeal, and that heat and irritability
of temper, by which the poffeffor is fitted, in fuit-
able conjunctures, and with adequate talents, to
fpread the flames of war, and to promote Revo-
lutions in the world. Thomas Paine is unlearn-
ed; but nature has given him a ftrong, though
coarfe, underftanding, with much originality of
thought and energy of expreffion. He is fitted by
nature to be a democratic Leader; and early prejudice, habit, and a variety of accidental circumftances, confirmed the original tendency of his
mind. Edmund Burke has had the advantage of

a

a learned education: His genius is showy, but
not solid; copious, but not correct. His judgment is inferior to that of many of his co-
temporaries; but he unites induſtry with wit,
humour, and a brilliant, though diſordered,
imagination: His elocution is rapid, and well
adapted to the ſportive or impetuous ſtyle of
oratory in which he excels; but he is ſeldom ar-
gumentative, and more ſeldom convincing. Had
literature been his profeſſional purſuit, he might
have ſhone through many a volume a ſplendid,
ſuperficial Rhetorician, decked in the ornaments
of a glittering eloquence, and proud of his tinſel.
For philoſophical reſearch, his faculties are leſs
fit; and in the more abſtruſe ſciences he probably never could have diſcovered one important
truth; but, like Fontenelle, he might have explained what others had invented, and might
have embelliſhed the ſyſtem of Newton with wit,
pathos, and all the tinkling trappings of his me-
taphorical ſtyle. But he was doomed to be a
politician; and the pride of genius and learning
fitted him to be an ariſtocrat. Early connection
with an honoured Nobleman confirmed this natural and acquired tendency; he was at firſt his
dependent; then, freed from that ſervitude by
his noble Patron's munificence at his death, he
became the counſellor and confidential guide of
an alarmed ariſtocracy. At the period alluded
to, the popular ſocieties for Reform had received
a rapid increaſe: The grateful zealot of ariſtocracy trembled with rage and fear at the approaching ruin of their uſurpations. But one
great effort to ſave them muſt be made; and,
for-

fortunately for his purpofe, the exceffes of the French Revolution held out a confoling hope that the fyftem of abufes might be prolonged, perhaps perpetuated. He defcribed thofe exceffes, and predicted more, in the tragic colours of an eloquence but too well fuited to their enormity; and events ftill gratified his humanity with the fulfilment of his predictions. On this occafion, the rafh Republican who had before denied that we have a Conftitution, ftept forth a fecond time into the field of combat, and, in his rage for confufion, propofed an Agrarian tax for England, holding forth to the poor the plunder of the rich. This was the very act of folly and temerity which his ariftocratic antagonift probably wifhed; and now Burke, with the united ariftocracy at his back, called with impetuous vociferation for a crufade againft France, and the dormancy of our Conftitution. This was the critical period of Mr Pitt's adminiftration. If the Minifter, at that time, had firmly oppofed each of thefe combuftible politicians; if he had fecured the peace of the country againft the wild projects of Paine, and refifted the counfels of Burke, as wild, and in the event far more pernicious, he would have been the greateft benefactor to the country and to mankind. He might, indeed, have been turned out of his official fituation; but the unanimous voice of a grateful public would foon have recalled him to it, with full power to carry into effect thofe neceffary plans of Reformation with which his political courfe had been begun. Inftead of thus mounting to the fummit of true glory, and thero

placing

placing himfelf on a level with Wafhington, he was difcouraged by the fhort difficulties of the afcent; he chofe to defcend from the eminence he had attained, and to keep the undifturbed poffeffion of the firft feat at the Board of Trea-fury. Sound policy required him to hold a middle courfe between the two dangerous ex-tremes of Paine and Burke. But Burke's vio-lence in the Senate for a war with France was not ill adapted to the new fyftem of the Minif-ter, and it gradually appeafed their long hoftili-ty. Inftead of fhunning each of thefe inflamma-tory men, he flew from the turbulent Republi-can to embrace the factious Enthufiaft of the Ariftocracy. To the wildeft flights of Burke's maddening imagination he nodded approba-tion; and Burke declared himfelf much dulcified to him. Soon after that, negociation, humbly and repeatedly fought by the Government of France, was proudly rejected by the Englifh Mi-nifter; the military force by fea and land was rapidly augmented, and nothing but a pretext feemed wanting for an immediate commence-ment of hoftilities. But when war is refolved on, a pretext can never be long wanted. The pretext found, was the death of Louis the Six-teenth, after a declaration in the Englifh Parlia-ment that peace or war fhould be the confequence of the pardon or execution of that Monarch. On this unjuft interference depended a queftion which involved the fate of a great part of man-kind. The declaration haftened the death of the unfortunate Monarch it was meant to fave, and that event to the Englifh Cabinet was decifive

for

for war; and yet high authority has not fcrupled to call it a juft and neceffary war.

It is true that the determination for war was not without fome pretence of provocation to this country; but it was fuch provocation as our own conduct had excited, and fuch as a Wafhington would have pardoned in a nation ftruggling for liberty, inflamed and almoft diftracted in the paroxyfm of a revolutionary fever. His humane and prudent policy might have taught the Minifter not to have fought pretexts for war, but to have fhunned them; to have been prepared for defence, but to have maintained neutrality; and to have tried every expedient of patience and temperate negociation to have preferved the peace of his country. Such was the actual conduct of the wife Statefman of America under fimilar or greater provocations from France; and fuch would have been the counfel of Burke, if he had been cool, difinterefted, and wife like Wafhington. But the character of our penfioned Politician is the very reverfe; in his temper, paffionate and fiery; in his purfuit of power and emolument, eager and indefatigable; in his public counfels, rafh and violent: his claims to the honours of a true Patriot or a wife Statefman will be difallowed by pofterity. In public life he has neither been independent nor difinterefted. Before the French Revolution, the general tenor of his conduct was little ufeful to his country; after that event, it has been pernicious both to his country and to the general interefts of humanity.

Unfortunately, the Minifter preferred the furious

rious fuggeftions of a paffionate Declaimer to the example of Wafhington's juft and humane policy; poffibly, too, the unjuft and delufive hope to difmember France and aggrandize Great-Britain might contribute to miflead him. The avowed purpofe of the war, at leaft it was avowed by the Minifter's new advifer, was to perpetuate the eftablifhed fyftem of abufes; to beat down and for ever fupprefs the *Jacobinical* principles of Locke and Sidney, of Savile and Chatham.—— And what has been the refult of this war, fo eagerly commenced, on views fo juft and reafonable? An unprecedented expence of blood and treafure; a long feries of difafters, intermixed with fuccefles few and inadequate; impending famine; approaching bankruptcy; and an aggravation of national difcontent, accompanied with unequivocal proofs, perfonally applied to the Minifter, of the anger and refentment of the people. The fyftem of war and coercion, inftead of appeafing the popular difcontents, has been found to inflame them; and the clamours of a ftarving populace have daily refounded louder and louder in the ears of Majefty for Peace and a Reform of Parliament.

5. But hence have been furnifhed frefh pretexts to the Minifter for his enterprizes againft the rights and liberty of his country. To ftifle thefe complaints, the galling cord of coercion has been ftrained with augmented rigour, and fuddenly the people have found themfelves expofed, by a new and fevere ftatute, to *vague and conftructive charges of Treafon;* and by another act, more dangerous ftill, deprived of their an-

cient

cient and indubitable right to *Free Difcuſſion* and
Free Petition. In vain was it pleaded by the
advocates of thefe rights, that, for the fault of
a few defperate individuals, innocent millions
ought not, and juſtly could not, forfeit their undoubted rights; in vain was it pleaded, that, as
far as human laws can proteƈt them, the ancient
law of the land was clearly fufficient to proteƈt
his Majeſty's Perfon and Government; that to
violate the privileges of the people, folemnly ſti-
pulated for them at the Revolution, and confirmed by the Bill of Rights, was a procedure
big with injuſtice and danger; that a precedent
thus trenching on that fundamental law had a
manifeſt tendency to unfettle the Government,
and if not quickly reverfed by Parliament, on
the remonſtrances of an injured and indignant
people, would lead by certain confequence either to confuſion, or the fpeedy extirpation of
our liberties. The influence of the Miniſter of
Reform prevailed; the injurious Bills were paffed; the people were reſtrained in the exercife
of their right to petition, and by this privation
the only rational ground of hope was loſt, that a
peaceful interpoſition of the people might effeƈt
a Reformation of Parliament. By a vigorous
exertion the nation may recover thefe loſt rights,
and with them reſtore the profpeƈt of a future redrefs of their other grievances; but after this
conduƈt of the Miniſter, no change of meafures
can reſtore to him the loſt eſteem and confidence
of the public. Let Mr Pitt's moſt partial friends
now declare, whether his hoſtility to Reform be
ſtill problematical; or, whether the tenor of his
conduƈt

conduct has not clearly demonftrated that he is become an enemy to that neceffary meafure.

This is the material point in the prefent Cafe; it is the hinge on which the judgment of his judges will turn, either to approve or cenfure the conduct of the Truftee. If this point be clearly eftablifhed, as he hopes it is, objections drawn from the temper of the times can have little weight to diffuade the publication. It is not his intention to aggravate faults, or to inflame difcontent: the faults have been committed, and the difcontent has been excited; and it is his purpofe to demonftrate thofe faults, in order only that they may be corrected; to evince the juftice of the popular complaint, only that it may be redreffed; and to point out the approaching danger, only that it may be avoided. He wifhes to imprefs on the perfons chiefly concerned, what he conceives to be inconteftible truths; that it were better and wifer to endeavour to conciliate than to crufh the people; that it were more juft, more humane, and fafer too, to make feafonable and prudent conceffions, than to attempt to fupprefs the fpirit of Reform by the ftrong hand of military power. Conceffion may fecure the public tranquillity, and augment the public happinefs; the attempt to compel fubmiffion without redrefs would be equally ruinous whether, in the fatal conteft that muft enfue, the people were victors or overcome. Before the war with France took place, he forefaw that the fyftem fo vehemently preffed by the zealot of ariftocracy could tend to nothing but an aggravation of the then exifting difcontent, and

finally

finally to defperation and national confufion. In
his public Letter to Mr Pitt, he ftated thefe evils
as the too probable confequence of a great foreign war, and an internal fyftem adverfe to the
rights of the people. In the progrefs of this unfortunate war, and in the evolution of this unpo-
pular fyftem, their calamitous confequences have
but too plainly and diftinctly verified the former
part of his prediction ; and aggravated difcontent
now threatens that cataftrophe which every good
citizen muft deprecate and wifh to avert. In
this perilous ftate of the country, he wifhes to
afk men in power, Shall we perfevere in the meafures which have manifeftly produced this alarming change in the temper of the people? Shall we
perfevere in this fatal war, contending at every
poffible rifque for advantages; fome of which are
ideal, fome may be more fubftantial, but are evidently unattainable? Shall we perfevere in the
fyftem of internal coercion, protecting acknowledged abufes, and advancing with hafty ftrides,
like ravifhers in open day, to invade the rights of
the people, and violate the proftrate Conftitution?
Is it thus we expect to fecure the tranquillity of
the country, by leaving the great mafs of the
community no property to lofe, and no privilege
which they can think fecure? In this dangerous
crifis, is it the part of a faithful fubject and real
well-wifher to his country to diffemble grievances; to acquiefce under the dangerous policy of
the new fyftem, and fuffer a daring Minifter to
go on, unwarned, heaping mifery upon mifery,
till the veffel of national patience be filled and
run over? Or, is it not rather truly becoming
that

that character, to raise his voice, however feeble it may be, and to beseech and adjure the Representatives of the nation to return to the ways of peace and safety; to exert their constitutional powers to close the unjust and fatal contest with France; and to redress with moderation and prudence, before it be too late, those great and acknowledged grievances of which the public complain? There was in the year 1780 more violent fermentation in the minds of the lower classes of the people, and it burst out in acts of more extensive and dangerous outrage than those which have been witnessed at this time. Indolent, and perhaps timid, as Lord North was, he resisted the demands of an intolerant populace, and he did well. He was nobly supported in it by Sir G. Savile and other wise Patriots of that day: With all their regard for the sense of the people, with all their condescension for their prejudices, they felt the disgrace which must attend their yielding to the barbarous wish of intolerance; they felt they had acted aright in extending toleration, and they generously resolved to brave the popular fury, and maintain the benevolent system they had established. The misguided people were ashamed of their unjust and intemperate conduct, and the just firmness of Parliament abashed intolerance for ever. But far different from the wisdom of that perseverance would be the resolution of Parliament to persist in supporting the new system of the Minister. The lower classes of the people may manifest symptoms of impatient discontent, against which the Executive Government ought to keep a vigilant guard; but the

F   Legis-

Legiflature is bound to appeafe that difcontent, if poffible, by lenient and conciliatory means.

It is, perhaps, among things poffible, that lenity and prudent conceffion might fail to foothe and pacify the people, and reftore perfect harmony and tranquillity to the country; but a bare poffibility of a failure is no fufficient reafon why the humane experiment fhould not firft be tried. If it fhould fucceed, a world of mifery would be faved; but till the effect of lenient meafures has been proved, a fyftem of coercion and reftraint is neither juft nor politic. It is unjuft to cavil at the cries of the people, and to refufe redrefs, becaufe it may be afked with impatience, in too loud a tone; it is in thefe times doubly impolitic to alienate their affections, when juftice is all they afk. The abufes which are complained of are real and moft pernicious abufes; the beft and wifeft men in the kingdom, with the Minifter himfelf at their head, have fanctioned their complaints, and propofed redrefs. The people are now contending againft ufurpations and abufes, the neceffary confequence of which, if uncorrected, muft be the lofs of public liberty, the depravation of public morals, and a Government fupported againft the virtue and good fenfe of the nation; firft, by corruption; at laft, by tyrannical force alone. Univerfal fuffrage may be an inadmiffible principle of Reform in the prefent ftate of this country, and immenfely numerous affemblies of the people may well excite fome apprehenfion of tumult; but to fupprefs thefe great affemblies by penal laws, and leave the difcontents of the people unappeafed by any redrefs,

may

may produce a fhort interval of calm, but it will foon be fucceeded by greater ftorms than ever. The means propofed by the people for effecting their end may be improper, but the end itfelf is good and laudable. To cut off confeffed abufes, and to deftroy corruption, they are fure muft be proper, and it is now their turn to feel they are right. The perfeverance of Parliament would not now abafh them; it would but increafe and exafperate their difcontent; and thus Parliament might too probably lofe their confidence for ever.

To prevent this fatal evil, and to fecure the genuine principles of the Conflitution, muft be the wifh of every good citizen. Except the few Patrons of Boroughs, Peers, and Commoners, who form an Ariftocracy which is unknown and hoftile to the Conftitution, all are interefted to promote a temperate Reform of thofe abufes which conftitute the power of that Ariftocracy. Some of thefe Peers and Commoners, on whom the chance of their birth has devolved a fhare in the unconftitutional powers alluded to, have nobly fet the example of preferring the juft fecurity of the people's rights to the retention of an odious and unjuft command. If aught of prudence or an honourable fhame, or a ftill more laudable feeling of benevolence, could induce a few of their brethren to renounce that iniquitous patronage, all might yet be well. Let the new fyftem of the Minifter be abandoned; let peace be concluded with France on equitable terms; let a Reformation of Parliament, on Mr Pitt's fafe and moderate plan, be granted, with a reftoration of our

F 2   ancient

ancient and indubtable right to free difcuffion and free petition, and the quiet and happinefs of the country will be effectually fecured. Thefe are the means, the only means, by which the nation may be reftored to that good temper on which the prefervation of its internal peace depends, and to that cordial efteem and veneration for its Government, in which, after the conclufion of a peace with France, the only juft and permanent fecurity can be found againft the increafing power of the French Republic, and againft the progrefs of their democratic principles.

The motives which have been affigned for the Truftee's fufpicion, and confequent breach with Mr Pitt, he is confident will not be queftioned by his honourable friends, on whofe account he firft thought of drawing this plea, in the anxious hope to obtain their acquittal and approbation : But, he doubts not, it will be faid by uncandid bigots, and mercenary adherents to the Minifter, that the breach, and the fubfequent publications, have been occafioned by pique and refentment. To this random objection it might be fufficient to return an anfwer when any particular caufe of offence were affigned, or any particular time were fixed when this pretended pique and refentment took place : But Mr Wyvill will not allow a furmife fo falfe the exiftence of a moment. He afferts, and he believes that Mr Pitt and his honourable friends are too juft not to confirm the affertion, that the conduct of Mr Wyvill in publifhing his correfpondence with Mr Pitt has not originated in any perfonal quarrel. No time can be fixed as
the

moment when any fuppofed offence was given; nor can any fort of incivility be fpecified, which it will not be eafy for Mr Wyvill to difprove. The conjecture has no foundation in fact, and is nothing more than an imaginary fuppofition. Mr Wyvill never received aught at the hands of Mr Pitt but perfonal civility, with many proofs of his efteem and regard. For thofe civilities, and for the efteem and confidence with which Mr Pitt was pleafed to honour him, he returned gratitude and affectionate attachment, increafed by high refpect for his political character. In his public demeanour, and in debate with his antagonifts, Mr Pitt may be lofty and daring; but in his deportment in private fociety there is much eafe and affability: He poffeffes a rich fund of benignity and good-nature; and it is not eafy to approach him in the freedom of friendly intimacy, without feeling a ftrong predilection for him. Mr Wyvill loved the Man, and looked up to the Minifter with reverence and veneration, as a truly Patriot Statefman, devoted to combat and deftroy the monftrous fyftem of corruption, and deftined to the high honour to be the political faviour of his country. In the eftimation of Mr Wyvill, his connection with Mr Pitt was the pride and honour of his life: But in the progrefs of his adminiftration, events occurred which infpired fome ferious fufpicions of his real intention and views, and gradually lowered this lofty idea of his character. Confidence in a pure and exalted character is a pleafing fenfation; it is always quitted with reluctance; and the beginning of this diftruft was,

to

to the writer, matter of deep regret and mortification. A painful struggle ensued between habitual prejudice and personal regard on the one side, and growing distrust and public duty on the other At last, by the farther unfolding of his new system, in the course of a few years, suspicion was gradually changed into conviction, duty overcame the united powers of prejudice and personal partiality, the connection with Mr Pitt was resigned, and the letter of Feb. 9, 1793, announcing this publication, was laid before the public.

From the same uncandid and mercenary quarters may be expected another surmise equally contrary to fact, and for which not the slightest appearance of probability can be pleaded. It will probably be said, that Mr Wyvill is a man chagrined by disappointment in his ambitious views through Mr Pitt; that his present conduct is dictated by the usual selfishness of politicians; that he wishes thus to recommend himself to new connections, and, by their assistance, to pursue more successfully his favourite objects, the acquisition of professional dignity, or the renewal of family honour. He does not affect to despise the honours of his profession; he does not pretend to think that the recovery of the rank long held by those who preceded him in the possession of his patrimony would be no benefit to his family: But these acquisitions have not been the objects of his ambition.

When he commenced his political course in Yorkshire, near seventeen years ago, some of the Gentlemen of this County, for whose public virtue

virtue and public views he feels the fincereſt refpect, were pleaſed to expreſs their confidence in
his integrity. His reply was, that he hoped
their confidence would remain undiminiſhed, as
long as his ſituation ſhould remain unchanged.
He is not totally unexperienced in the world, or
abſolutely ignorant of the ways and paſſages,
though often dark and intricate, by which pro-
motion may be moſt fuccefsfully attained. When
their confidence had opened to him the door of
advancement, he could have availed himſelf of
the opportunity, if to profit by his politics had
been his deſign. His viſible ſituation is now exactly what it was then; it is, in fact, the fame
ſituation. To this deciſive . circumſtance he
might truſt the fure, though ſilent, confutation
of the miſrepreſentation he has here anticipated.

But he wiſhes not to leave his innocence reſpecting the ſuppoſed imputation to be inferred
by the candour or lenity of his judges: His anfwer ſhall be direct and explicit. He aſſerts,
therefore, and once more he truſts Mr Pitt will
confirm the aſſertion, that he has never aſked or
accepted from him any favour, great or ſmall, either for himſelf or any of his friends. He might
juſtly extend the fame aſſertion to all the other
perſons in miniſterial ſtations with whom it has
been his fortune to have any intercourſe or connection. The ſuppoſed charge, therefore, that
his preſent conduct is the effect of chagrin and
diſappointment, muſt be altogether unfounded.

Mr Wyvill was aware, that there is in the beſt
of men a great portion of frailty and fallibility;
that the temptations to which they are expoſed

in

in public life are ſtrong and numerous, and that
the human heart is apt to be corrupted by the
long poſſeſſion of power. Of Mr Pitt's integrity and wiſdom his eſteem was high; but he
knew the extreme difficulty of the enterprife he
had undertaken : He knew his virtue would be
aſſailed by every poſſible temptation which the
Court and the Ariſtocracy could employ to inti-
midate or ſeduce him from his purpoſe; and
even Mr Pitt's virtue might yield to their temptations. It was poſſible that he might ſhrink
from the glorious taſk he had engaged in, and,
inſtead of perſevering in the ſtruggle to beſtow
on his country the ſecure enjoyment of its liberty, under a Government controuled by a reformed and virtuous Repreſentative of the People, he might turn his whole power and credit
to ſupport eſtabliſhed abuſes and corruptions.
He felt, therefore, that it was poſſible the im-
perious voice of duty might call upon him to renounce his connection, and to oppoſe him in the
proſecution of his new ſyſtem of Adminiſtration.
But obligation and independence are incompati-
ble; and public duty can only be performed
with unblemiſhed integrity by men who have
kept their minds free and uninfluenced by fa-
vours. He, therefore, determined to preſerve
his freedom and independence, by never min-
gling with the crowd of ſervile and ſelfiſh men,
who ſeek emolument or honours at the levees of
a Miniſter : He never ſtooped to ſolicit or accept
any miniſterial favour : He is, and always has
been, abſolutely free from obligation to the preſent Miniſter, and all his predeceſſors in power ;
and

and the refult of the freedom of judgment thus
preferved is the conduct which has been here
explained to the public.

But no proof of innocence can be fo clear and
cogent as to convince the enraged bigot, or re-
duce the hireling advocate of power to filence.
No mifreprefentation is too bold and daring for
the front of the hireling; no calumny is too
grofs and abfurd for the credulity of the bigot.
Even after the ftatement of thefe facts, the
charge of ambition probably will be repeated; but it will meet the filence of the injured
perfon, and the reprobation of impartial and
equitable men. They will have feen the proofs
of his probity; and, he trufts, they will not
fuffer the opinion eftablifhed on the firm foundation of thefe facts to be overturned by the
breath of rumour or idle furmife. Judging of
his prefent intention by his paft conduct, they
will not eafily credit the affertion, that he who
hitherto has fhunned the fnares of obligation
with fo much care, is now willing to entangle
himfelf in them; that the man fo jealous of his
independence, who long fupported the Minifter,
but never would be his partizan, is now feeking
to be the vaffal of fome new political chieftain,
and to facrifice the confcious pride of integrity
to the bafe views of a felfifh ambition. It is true
he honours the great Statefmen, and their co-
adjutors in each Houfe of Parliament, who have
oppofed the new fyftem of the Minifter: He ap-
proves their principles; he admires their talents;
he applauds their perfeverance; and, as far as
his flender means permit, he will co-operate
with

with them to fave the finking liberties of his
country. But he is not their follower or their
partizan; he is, and he will be, the partizan
and fervant to the public alone.

Such is the plea for *the paft* and *the intended
conduct* of the Writer refpecting Mr Pitt, and the
Paper which he intrufted to his cuftody. It is
conduct which has been haftily blamed by men,
whofe acquittal and approbation on this explanation of facts and their motives he ftill covets, and
is not without hope to obtain. But if, after this
ftatement, Mr Pitt's honourable friends alluded
to fhould retain their unfavourable opinion, it is
conduct which he will not regret, if men, partial
neither to the Minifter nor himfelf, fhall pro-
nounce his abfolution. To the judgment of an
impartial public, therefore, he commits his cafe;
and he awaits their decifion with refpect, but
without fear or purturbation. In the courfe of
political bufinefs in which he has been engaged,
he is confcious of having acted with integrity;
and on the prefent occafion it has been his moft
anxious endeavour to do his duty to the public,
and at the fame time to avoid all injuftice or
perfonal difrefpect to Mr Pitt. But it is poffible,
that, either from the ftrength of his zeal, or the
weaknefs of his judgment, he may have fallen
into fome error refpecting the nature of the truft
in queftion. He is abfolutely unconfcious of it,
and he hopes it has not really happened. But
if, in the judgment of candid, judicious, and
experienced men, he has been thus mifled, and
without impropriety cannot publifh the Paper in
queftion without the confent of Mr Pitt, he

is

is not inclined to controvert the judgment of such men, or to persist in his present intention against their decision. He will bow with deference to the authority ·of such men, and, in conformity with their opinion, will postpone the intended publication : And, he trusts, that with them the rectitude of his intention may plead his excuse for unperceived and involuntary error. But if he has been fortunate enough to convince them that he holds that Paper in trust for the public, and that, under the circumstances stated, he has a right to publish it, their opinion will confirm his own, and he will, without delay, produce the Paper in dispute.

In times like the present it cannot be dangerous to draw the attention of the public to the mild, but effectual, plan of Reformation proposed by Mr Pitt in the purer period of his Administration. It was then proposed, because it was thought expedient to allay the just dissatisfaction of the people : It is more expedient now, because their discontent is greater ; it has been increased by delay and disappointment, and nothing but redress can terminate with safety the present fermentation. It is the disposition to refuse redress which is dangerous, not the statement of moderate terms on which it may be prudent to ask it, nor the resolution to·concede when such terms are asked by an aggrieved people. The plan proposed by Mr Pitt would be safe for every class and order in the State, more especially for those on whom the dread of innovation may be supposed to operate with greatest power. It would be safe for the Crown; it
would

would be fafe for the Peerage alfo: it would
check the tendency to Republican principles; it
would refcind the ufurpations of a factitious, il-
legal, and felf-created Ariftocracy, which now
domineers over all the conftituted Authorities;
it would reftore the Peerage to its juft dignity,
as the true and honoured Ariftocracy of the
land; and by rendering the Commons Houfe of
Parliament a fair Reprefentative of the nation,
it would free the Monarchy from the fhackles of
an unconftitutional cabal, and at once content
the people, and fecure the permanence of a
juftly-limited monarchical Government. It is a
plan calculated to avert the impending dangers
of anarchy and defpotifm; to protect, with equal
energy, the property and the liberty of the country; and to preferve alike the internal peace and
the conftitutional rights of the community, under
the incorruptible guard of a reformed and virtuous Reprefentation.

C. WYVILL.

APPEN-

APPENDIX.

Paper I.

Letter *from the* Rev. C. WYVILL *to the* Rev.
JAMES WILKINSON.

NEROT'S HOTEL, KING-STREET, ST JAMES'S,
Dec. 9, 1784.

Dear Sir,

I Hope Mr Shore has had an opportunity to
fhew you my firft Letter, in which I gave
him an account of what paffed moft material in
my converfation with Mr Pitt on Monday. By
appointment, I faw him again yefterday, and had
another long and very confidential converfation
with him. I truft you think I have not been
hafty in giving my efteem to Minifters, or too
apt to vouch for the integrity of their intentions. But, on this occafion, I feel I fhould act a
mean and an ungenerous part if I did not moft
explicitly declare, that if I had entertained any
doubt before, refpecting Mr Pitt's zeal for the
public caufe, which I certainly did not, thefe
converfations muft have convinced me of the
purity of his political character, and his fincere
and particular attachment to the caufe of Parliamentary Reformation. I have not the fmalleft
doubt

doubt that he will exert himfelf to the utmoft of his ftrength in the approaching Seffion of Parlia- ment, and put forth his whole power and credit *as a Man* and *as a Minifter*, *honeftly* and *boldly* to carry a plan of Reform, by which our liber- ties will be placed on a footing of permanent fecurity. I am happy to add, the profpect of fuccefs is improved beyond our utmoft expecta- tions.

In confequence of this fecond converfation, the idea I expreffed to Mr Shore, of the propriety, and even neceffity, of a County Meeting for Yorkfhire this winter, is much confirmed. It is due not only to the public caufe, and to that confiftency of character which every man of ho- nour wifhes to preferve, but in juftice alfo to a Minifter, who, for the public good, is refolved to act fo nobly difinterefted a part.—I have only time to add,

> I am ever, my dear Sir,
> Moft cordially your's,
> C. WYVILL.

Paper II.

Paper II.

LETTER *from the* Rev. C. WYVILL *to* General
HALE.

NEROT'S HOTEL, KING-STREET, ST JAMES'S,
Dec. 13*th*, 1784.

My dear General,

NOTWITHSTANDING our very unlucky
diverfity of fentiment upon one queftion
of very inferior moment, I cannot entertain a
moment's doubt but the intelligence I have to
communicate will be moft agreeable to you.

Before I left England, which, for reafons you
probably may have heard, I had intended doing
for fome months, I thought it due to the common caufe to wait upon Mr Pitt. I faw him on
Monday and Wednefday laft: On both thofe
days I had much confidential converfation with
him, refpecting his ideas of Parliamentary Reformation, and the moft advifeable means of effecting it. But, confidential as it was, I think myfelf authorized to declare to you, that he will
moft certainly bring his Propofitions on early in
the next Seffion; that he will fupport them to
the utmoft of his ftrength, and put forth his
whole power and credit, *as a Man* and *as a Minifter*, *honeftly* and *boldly*, to carry fuch a meliorated fyftem of Reprefentation as may place the
Conftitution on a footing of permanent fecurity.
I am happy to add, that the profpect of fuccefs
is

is improved much beyond our moſt ſanguine expectations.

If, in conſequence of this encouraging intelligence, Gentlemen ſhould think of meeting at
York this winter, in order to give their ſupport
to a meaſure ſo beneficial to the country, I
ſhould be ſorry to be abſent. Here, therefore,
I mean to ſtay till the queſtion be aſcertained,
whether a County Meeting will be held this winter in Yorkſhire. Before this converſation with
Mr Pitt, I had uniformly and ſtrenuouſly declared my opinion to all our friends with whom
I had an opportunity to converſe, that after his
declaration in the Houſe of his intention to agitate the ſubject this winter, we are bound by
every tie of public duty and regard to private
character, and that conſiſtency we all wiſh to
maintain, to endeavour to call the County together to ſupport the meaſure; and however irk-
ſome and inconvenient it may be to me perſon-
ally to attend, no ſuppoſable degree of fatigue
or inconvenience ſhall deter me from once more
joining thoſe friends, with whom I am proud to
have acted ſo long, in behalf of the common
cauſe. I beg my beſt compliments to your La-
dies;   And am, with great reſpect,
                    Dear General,
              Your moſt ſincere and faithful
                    humble ſervant,
                         C. WYVILL.

Paper III.

Paper III.

Letter *from the* Rev. C. WYVILL *to* Sir THOMAS
DUNDAS (*now* Lord DUNDAS).

NEROT'S HOTEL, KING-STREET, St JAMES'S,
Dec. 20*th*, 1784.

Dear Sir,

AFTER having performed, in fome tolerable
degree, what my duty to the Yorkfhire
Committee required, I now take the earlieft opportunity to communicate to you the refult of
my late interview with Mr Pitt.

After much converfation on the fubject of
Parliamentary Reformation, he authorized me to
affert, that he means to bring that fubject before
the Houfe of Commons as foon as poffible in the
next Seffions; that he will fupport his intended
propofitions to the utmoft of his ftrength, and
exert his whole power and credit *as a Man* and
as a Minifter, honeftly and *boldly,* to carry fuch a
meliorated fyftem of Reprefentation, as may
place the Conftitution on a footing of permanent
fecurity.

If the true Britifh fpirit of liberty fhould be
roufed in Yorkfhire, as I truft it will, by a declaration like this, and a County Meeting fhould
be called in order to fupport fo neceffary a meafure, I truft we fhall have the fupport of Sir
Thomas Dundas; whom I have long confidered
as one of the moft zealous and truly difinterefted
friends to the propofed Reform, and by whofe
kind

kind affiftance, principally, that unanimity which
alone can render fuch a Meeting effectual may
be preferved.

I am, dear Sir, with great refpect,

Your moft faithful, humble fervant,

C. WYVILL.

FINIS.